13 FALMOUTH ROAD

A DCI CLAIRE CORNISH

MYSTERY

F G LAYCY

The door to 13 Falmouth Road had a lot to say. People entered, and people left, but they were never the same again

Table of Contents

Preface

Some people believe the number thirteen is bad luck. They say it's unlucky to have thirteen guests at a dinner party and many buildings don't have a thirteenth floor. Being born or getting married on this day is considered unfavourable. And buying a house with this number is deemed jinxed bringing chaos and evil.

That is precisely what happened to the unfortunate occupants and persons associated with the sale of 13 Falmouth Road, Truro. If you were to stroll down Falmouth Road and observe the grand terraced houses in all their glory, you wouldn't think that this particular house held ill-fated secrets inside. To the outside world, the house looked like any other on the street. A picture of safety and strength, with its black door to countenance and ward off harm. But this was a cloak, to shield the truth behind its ominous entrance that was unleashed on that fateful date. And the catalyst for the rest to come.

Estate agents Abbott & Abbott had cornered the market over the last twenty-five years in Cornwall. Dealing with the wealthiest clients who purchased prime waterfront, and country and townhouses in the Southwest.

They had personally handled sales on this particular street at an average value of one million pounds.

It would probably astound estate agents, especially Abbott & Abbott, to discover how many people hated them. Considering they sold their clients their prospective dream home. It wasn't just a slight dislike. This hatred was a big-time fury. For some people, their disdain for the estate agents Abbott & Abbott was a truly deep-rooted hatred. Unfortunately, some of that hatred was justified. And some of that hatred was aimed at those in the firing line.

But there was more to it than that. A lot more.

Chapter One

The Cornish Guardian had placed the notification as per the anonymous letter received. The payment had been in cash and was therefore untraceable.

A murder is announced and will take place on Saturday 3 November 2018, at the Halloween Masked Ball, Holland House, Truro.

Detective Chief Inspector (DCI) Claire Cornish and Detective Sergeant (DS) Gary Pearce walked into the resplendent Holland House, a gothic style manor house on the outskirts of Truro, and rather apt for a Halloween Masked Ball. The ball was an invitation-only function, and Detective Chief Superintendent (DCS) Danielle Butler, had pulled a few strings to obtain a couple of invitations without drawing attention. Only the organiser of the ball knew that two undercover police officers would be present. He didn't know why, except that they were there to observe the guests.

Pearce looked at Cornish.

'You look beautiful tonight. It's a pity Jamie isn't here with you. You'll just have to put up with me,' Pearce winked.

'You're not so bad yourself. You scrub up pretty well,' Cornish said quietly so no one else could hear.

Cornish was wearing a scarlet dress, without a corset, so she could breathe, and a mask to match. The whole ensemble against her porcelain skin was a dramatic change to her usual attire. Claire Cornish looked the picture of beauty and had been quite categorical that she didn't want a big princess dress but rather one she could move in and eat the four-course menu. It was rare that she had the opportunity to devour a meal of such quality, especially while on duty. The finished product was a lightweight combination of tulle, satin organza and taffeta, made for twirling and looking as though it was made for a princess.

Pearce wore a black and royal blue velvet print embroidered aristocratic coat and black tights to complement Cornish. And the requisite mask. He felt ridiculous in his outfit.

Cornish laughed.

'I think you look rather dashing.'

Jamie Nance, Claire's boyfriend, let out a whistle as he dropped off his fiancée and Pearce for the ball. He felt slightly envious that he couldn't attend, but it was business, not pleasure. And, if the announcement was anything to go by, someone intended to commit murder. Jamie stiffened. He wouldn't relax until Claire was safe and back home. She was a good policewoman who risked her own life to protect others. And no matter how well trained, and experienced his fiancée was, there was always that possibility that she could get injured. Jamie knew Claire wasn't alone, but that still didn't stop him worrying.

Cornish and her team had only just finished dealing with the fallout from another murder case. This was the last thing Cornish wanted. Another murder on her patch.

The guests gathered in the main hall engulfed by gothic décor, ornate and elegant and opulent. Several double doors off the hallway revealed the other rooms each embodying a different colour palette. The walls were papered in vibrant and dramatic colours, emerald green, ruby red and dark ocean blue. The fabrics were bold and made of silk or velvet. Decadence was the key as chandeliers gleamed from the ceilings. The décor was all about drama, and Cornish hoped the evening wouldn't end with a dramatic murder as announced in the Cornish Guardian.

Cornish and her team had very little time to prepare for the event. The organiser, Callum Roberts, had sent over the list of expected guests before to the event. Cornish and her team had gone through the invitees, but no one stood out. Callum Roberts recognised DCI Cornish from her picture in the papers.

'I'm so pleased you could come. I do hope there isn't a murder tonight, for all our sakes. I'm sorry we haven't had an opportunity to meet in person before tonight, but an event like this takes some planning.'

Cornish smiled as Callum Roberts continued.

'Holland House is impressive, don't you think, Detective Inspector?'

It was more of a rhetorical statement than a question.

'Do you have any idea who might want to commit murder here tonight? All our guests are very important people in the community.'

Callum Roberts' attitude would win him no brownie points with Cornish. He was clearly a closet snob who liked to rub shoulders with the right people. Cornish observed Roberts as he issued a string of demands to his staff before answering him.

'I'm afraid not at this moment in time, Mr Roberts. It may simply be a hoax.'

'Let's hope so. Help yourselves to champagne,' Callum Roberts replied, as he dismissed the police officers and turned to greet the other guests arriving that he considered more important.

Cornish had met plenty of people like Callum Roberts before, every unbearable type of Londoner, and they all made her toes curl. Some, like Callum Roberts, had migrated south to Cornwall. Once they were here, they insisted on talking about how much they didn't miss the city, yet they still wanted the social trappings that came with their old life. The Callum Roberts of the world grated with their patronising tone. Cornish was infuriated that this brusque man had so quickly got under her skin.

Cornish and Pearce followed the signs directing them to the reception room laid out for dinner. Place cards had been set for each guest. Cornish found herself sitting next to a rotund gentleman who continuously stared at her breasts as he spoke. Pearce was seated next to a lady of a similar age and appeared engrossed in conversation.

Cornish swept her eyes over the guests. She knew there were eighty people present and several high profile invitees. She recognised a retired pop star who used to adorn her walls, and his other half, who was also in a favourite girl band. Cornish thought the woman had fared much better with age, while he now resembled the average bald man in his late fifties. Life hadn't been particularly kind to him. Too much sun damage from a life spent surfing. And, to think he had been a heartthrob in his heyday. Cornish figured it couldn't be easy seeing yourself decline in the public eye.

Cornish was well aware that the other guests with them were well known. And connected. A retired footballer she didn't recognise. And his inconsequential wife who looked good on his arm. Elliot Abbott & Maxwell Abbott, estate agents, were among their party. Cornish suspected they were all clients of Abbott & Abbot at some time. Why else would the prestigious estate agents receive an invite?

The Rotary Club was present, in force, with a large contingency of members who were mainly professionals from the medical field, horticulture, business and advertising. Then there were a couple of landowners, farmers, who had struck it rich by having farmland on the Roseland Peninsula. All in all, an eclectic mix.

Cornish found herself enjoying the dinner, which somewhat surprised her. The company was lively and witty and as the wine flowed the tongues loosened. Cornish listened to the conversations going back and forth across the table. Most of the guests were acquainted and had met up at some time or other. Pearce was under instruction to do the same. At the head of the table, Callum Roberts gave a speech before the dessert course was served and the guests then moved into the other resplendent reception rooms.

After dinner, the guests mingled, relaxing in the piano room with an after-dinner drink or dancing in the elegant ballroom. The waiters were kept busy, and the two sommeliers discreetly opened the special reserve wines for their discerning guests.

Cornish thought to herself it was always the Butler who was the

murderer in mystery books. She hoped this evening would turn

out to be uneventful.

Cornish noticed there was a two-tier wine service. Even in this

rich circle, there appeared to be an unspoken hierarchy. The party

with Elliot Abbott & Maxwell Abbott were top of the softly

established pecking order with the farmers at the bottom. Cornish

was under no illusion. The rich and famous who attended these

events were a breed apart. She was a civilian and a DCI. She

noted the slight frisson between the ones that considered

themselves celebrities and the other guests.

The last of the diners had left the dining area and moved into one

of the other reception rooms. Cornish stood in the corner of the

piano room while Pearce stayed alert in the ballroom.

Cornish was beginning to think the whole thing was a hoax when

the ballroom was suddenly plunged into darkness.

Callum Roberts reassured the guests.

'It's alright, ladies and gentlemen. We get occasional power cuts.
Don't be alarmed. The power will be back on in a minute.'

It was inevitable that the power cut would make people confused,
disorientated. It was like being in a fog where you couldn't see in
front of you. Guests stumbled and bumped into one another,
knocking furniture in their panic. Cornish adjusted her eyes to the
darkness and shadows, the hairs on the back of her neck prickled.

Pearce placed a hand on her shoulder.

'Are you alright?'

'I'm fine. I think someone just flipped the fuse if I'm not
mistaken.'

The power returned almost immediately, and Cornish heard the
shrieks as the body of a man lay on the ballroom floor, with a
knife protruding from his back. It was a horrific sight; it was just

the blood. There was so much of it. The man's wife, Marie Abbott, fainted into the arms of her brother-in-law, Maxwell Abbott. Cornish knew the exact time of death.

Pearce was first on the scene. Cornish was next, stopping beside the body to feel for a pulse. She risked contaminating the crime scene, but the man may have been alive, if only barely. There was no pulse. The scene could have been mistaken for a mock Agatha Christie re-enactment. But this was no play, only foul play.

Cornish recognised the victim, Elliot Abbott. She needed to take control and get the attention of everyone. Her voice reverberated around the walls.

'Please listen, everybody, I regret to inform you that there has been a serious incident. Elliot Abbott has died. I'm DCI Cornish, and this is DS Pearce. The rest of the unit are on their way, but nobody is to leave. You will all be required to give a statement. Thank you.'

Cornish looked among the faces of the guests, a mixture of tears and stunned disbelief. Marie Abbott had been escorted to the music room, and the doctor was on his way. Cornish didn't want her being moved too far from the scene of the crime.

Callum Roberts pushed through the gathered bodies surrounding the dead man to see what had happened.

'He's dead Mr Roberts. Elliot Abbott is dead,' snapped Cornish.

'What do you mean, dead?' exclaimed Callum Roberts. It was inconceivable.

'Precisely that.'
Cornish wasn't used to having to explain herself very often and having her authority questioned. Callum Roberts quickly composed himself. He intended to place himself firmly in charge of the situation. Still, before he had a chance, Cornish stepped forward to prevent Callum Roberts from touching the body.

'The party is over Mr Roberts,' said Cornish brusquely.

The other guests were starting to get agitated. No one wanted to be associated with murder. Mutterings could be heard, and a spokesman for the party with Abbott & Abbott stepped forward to speak.

'If you think we're going to sit around here all night, you are mistaken.'

Cornish regarded the party of eight silently for a moment before giving a smile that didn't quite reach her eyes.

'In case you hadn't noticed this is now a murder enquiry, Mr Smith. I don't suppose Elliot Abbott, a friend and associate of yours, had any idea he would die this evening. Do you or any of the others in your party have somewhere more important to be? I suggest you assist the police with our enquiries.'

The gentleman in question was using an alias. Why Cornish couldn't figure out. Was it for the benefit of the press, because it certainly wasn't for the other guests? She knew who he was, and while she would humour him, with his fake name, nothing was going to get in the way of her murder enquiry.

Cornish glared at the party. They would toe the line, or she was quite prepared to cite them for obstruction and haul them down to the station. She was in no mood for games.

'I won't keep you here any longer than is absolutely necessary.'

Cornish put a call through to Lucy Turner, the Senior Crime Scene Investigator, attached to Devon and Cornwall. The next call was to DCS Danielle Butler, followed by CC, Chief Constable Jane Falconbridge. She would want to be informed regardless of the hour. Cornish had requested that she keep her Chief Constable updated of any events no matter how trivial. Cornish didn't trust Butler. There was no love lost between the two women. DCS Butler had only been in charge a short time, and the two women had already exchanged harsh words. Their working relationship wasn't going to be plain sailing. Cornish had previously complained about her superior to CC Jane Falconbridge. She had advised her to not pursue her grievance through the official channels. Cornish was now stuck with her immediate boss, for the time being.

Lucy Turner and Emma Bray arrived almost together. Bray was the CO, Assistant Coroner, and she formally established that Elliot Abbott was dead. At the same time, Turner, SOCO, and her team secured the area. Dressed up in the requisite white PPE (personal protective equipment) suits, nitrile gloves and head caps, the spotlight was erected to cast more brightness over the area. The chandeliers above gave limited light.

Cornish had instructed Pearce to make sure no guests left the premises and gathered in the piano room and the dining area, which had now been cleared. Cornish told Callum Roberts to make sure all staff stayed until they had been questioned and their whereabouts at the time of the murder had been established, and hopefully verified. Cornish wanted everyone to voluntarily consent to have a DNA swab for the purposes of elimination. She hoped no one would kick up a fuss.

While Cornish was engaged with another agitated guest, Turner tapped on her shoulder.

'I think you should see this,' and she handed Cornish the piece of paper found in Elliot Abbott's pocket. The handwritten note said simply,

'I'm here to take back what's mine.'

Chapter Two

Cornish instructed DS Hutchens and DC Mac as soon as they arrived to take down statements. It was going to be a long night, and the rest of the unit had been called in to assist.

Cornish watched Turner and Bray at work before remarking. 'Sorry to have dragged you both out on a Saturday night. I bet your other halves aren't too happy?'

Turner and Bray laughed. Cornish had no idea. Literally. Turner broke the ice.
'We're a couple. We thought you might have cottoned on to that fact ages ago. Have been for the last eighteen months.'

It was Cornish's turn to act surprised. She exchanged a glance with Pearce, who simply shrugged his shoulders. He had known about the relationship. Momentarily lost for words, Cornish couldn't believe she had missed the signs. There was no awkwardness as Cornish spoke.

'Well, that answers why you always turn up together. Mystery solved, and I must say I'm pleased, delighted.'

Turner continued her task taking a series of photographs of their dead man with her expensive camera. Cornish wanted her to take pictures of everyone, in all the rooms, so she could remember where everybody roughly was after the death. People behaved very differently after a crime, and that might offer up some clues as to who was responsible. Cornish had used her mobile to take shots at the time the body was discovered, as a starting point of reference.

'It was a bugger to work the crime scene,' said Lucy Turner, the senior CSI, when she caught up with Cornish. Time of death, as you stated, and indeed was present for, was 10.30 pm. The whole area was covered in prints. I need to establish who was where once we have confirmed all the impressions at the scene. The victim appears to have died from a single knife wound. Once Gilbert has him on the slab, he'll be able to tell you more. Murder is a nasty messy business. I'll be glad to see the back of this year.'

Cornish couldn't agree more.

Gary Gilbert, the forensic pathologist, would be ready and waiting to do the PM, post-mortem, back at base, on Monday morning. In unusual fashion, he was away for the weekend with his girlfriend. The relationship was in the early stages, but from what Cornish could see, love was very much in the air. Elliot Abbott would have to remain on ice until then.

All the guests had given their statements to the police. It had been a long night. The majority of the guests in the other parties had merely found the whole experience inconvenient and rather distasteful, forcing disingenuous smiles and polite murmurs from anybody required to listen. They hoped they wouldn't be kept too long. The odd guest found the experience to be too much, and the caterwauling would have made them an excellent mourner at a funeral. Cornish observed the Abbott & Abbott party of eight with suspicion. Marie Abbott was being comforted by the women in the party. At the same time, the men appeared to be whispering amongst themselves. Cornish couldn't make out what was being said.

Elliot Abbott was dead, and from the consensus of the evening's audience, he'd been an average man at best who was rather too fond of his own voice.

Cornish walked over to the party to further reiterate the point made earlier.

'I would appreciate it if you would make yourselves available for further questioning should the need arise.'

'Is that really necessary, Detective Chief Inspector Cornish. Of course, we're all devastated by Elliot's death, but I don't see what any of us has to do with it.'

'I'm afraid it has everything to do with you all,' Mr Smith.'

The police lingered into the early hours, gathering as much information as possible from the guests. Cornish wanted to garner everything she could on the victim and those present. Often, when people were shocked and traumatised, they let slip useful snippets that they would normally prefer not to divulge or reveal. In the reality of daylight, people tended to clam up. While their emotions were raw, Cornish hoped her team would discover something of importance. As the last of the guests left, Cornish observed the remaining scene of carnage. Elliot Abbott had been a man of many faces. A father of three, a doting family man and a loving husband by the party of eight. All extolling the virtues of this wonderful man. Then there were the other comments from other guests. An arrogant bastard, an opportunist crook, a real estate agent with no scruples.

Callum Roberts was looking perturbed. He couldn't account for the total number of staff on duty to DS Pearce, as they often called in agency cover for events of this size. He didn't think DCI Cornish would be impressed.

While the police dealt with over-tired revellers and the inebriated, one person stole away before anyone noticed they had even been there. The figure, unrecognised and annoyed by that fact, scurried out the basement entrance of the property and disappeared as quickly and quietly as they had come.

Chapter Three

DCI Claire Cornish finally walked into Honeysuckle cottage at five o'clock in the morning. Jamie had eventually given up waiting and taken himself to bed. Claire slipped out of her clothes and curled up beside him. She needed to feel the warmth of his body. Despite the events of the evening, Claire snuggled up to Jamie and slept like a baby.

Claire opened her eyes three hours later to find Jamie smiling at her with a mug of tea in his hand.

'You sleep so soundly,' he purred as he kissed her gently on the lips.

Claire knew her mouth must taste and smell like the night before, and conscious of that fact, she slipped out of bed and into the bathroom to quickly freshen up. She could have done with staying in bed for longer, but that was wishful thinking. She had another murder to solve, and like the waves outside, the deaths were rolling in thick and fast lately.

Claire glanced at the time. It was early, too early for a Sunday morning, which was supposed to be a day of rest. Not for her, though. Jamie only had today off, and he would be heading back up to Bristol for the working week. They were counting down the days until he moved in permanently.

Claire hoped this brief look at her hectic life wouldn't put the kibosh on their relationship. If Jamie stayed the course, then Claire would consider him a saint. They had recently opened the channel of communication with their daughter, Bonnie. She had come back into their lives after all these years.

Claire had been persuaded to have Bonnie adopted. At sixteen, Claire was too young to have a baby, her parents claiming she would have struggled to bring up her daughter on her own. And it would have ruined her future. Claire and Jamie lost their daughter, and each other, for thirty years. They had now rekindled their relationship, and Claire and Jamie desperately wanted to meet Bonnie who felt the same. Claire didn't want this latest murder to overshadow their reunion.

Claire walked down the stairs to the smell of bacon and eggs being cooked on her stove. The range had seen plenty of use with Jamie's arrival. She smiled as she watched Jamie dish up breakfast wearing very little.

'I hope you are going to play nicely today. No throwing your teddies out of the pram,' he said as he took a sip of coffee.

Claire laughed as she cheekily replied.

'Well, Mr Nance, it looks like you will have to play all alone today.'

They sat and chatted about the Halloween Ball and the murder. It had been the very first ball Claire had ever been to, and she would remember it for all the wrong reasons. The costumes, hired, would be returned Monday morning, and Claire was now firmly back in the real world.

Jamie scooted Claire out of the door an hour later, long enough

for them to come together and remember why they were a couple.

Chapter Four

Pearce had walked into his little two-bedroomed house in the early hours of Sunday morning. There was no one waiting for him. He had bought the place following his divorce and home was now St Austell on a small cul-de-sac. The neighbours were quiet and kept to themselves. Pearce kicked off his shoes, grateful to be home. Like most divorcés, he had made an attempt to lose weight and get fit. His wife had badgered him for years to take better care of himself, but it took her leaving him before he changed his ways. With his confidence and trim looks restored, he had recently been out on a few dates. Still, so far he'd not found anyone he could even consider having a long term relationship with. But the saying was so very true. Getting in the sack was like riding a bike. He might be a bit rusty, but the cogs still worked, even if his technique required some polish and practice.

Claire had asked him to walk her down the aisle at her forthcoming wedding to Jamie. No actual date had been placed in the diary, but Spring had been mentioned. Pearce liked Jamie.

Cornish and Pearce were more than just work colleagues; they

were friends. In fact, Pearce considered Cornish, Hutchens and

Mac his closest friends. They lived, breathed and worked well

together. They made a good team.

DC Dave Mac was the newest member of the team and one of the

few LGBT police officers in the Devon and Cornwall Police. He

had proved to be a valuable member. After a rocky start with

Pearce chiding him about his sexuality, they had become firm

friends and work colleagues.

DS Alex Hutchens was old enough to be Cornish's daughter and

at the peak of her career. A brilliant officer, she had scored highly

in her sergeants' exam, and among the top one per cent in the

country. Cornish considered Hutchens a great asset to her team.

Cornish had read her personal file and felt empathy towards her.

Alex Hutchens life had been affected by her adoption and then

the death of her elderly parents two years earlier. She had no boyfriends or relationships to speak of except with her work colleagues. Alex Hutchens considered them her friends.

The only fly in the ointment was the recent appointment of DCS Danielle Butler. Ambitious and single, she ate her opponents for breakfast. Danielle Butler had stolen the only other person Claire Cornish had considered marrying years ago. And Claire considered it a high probability that Butler would do the same again given half a chance. Claire wouldn't put it past her. Their lives had interwoven for years since they first met in Chantmarle Police Training Centre, Dorset. Cornish had come first out of all the cadets and Butler had been peeved. And that was the start of Danielle Butler's obsession with Claire Cornish.

They were the same age give or take a few months but entirely different creatures. Danielle Butler was a snake in the grass waiting to bite her victims. She collected weak souls. Butler took no prisoners, and her steely appearance with her short black hair and chisel features was as ruthless as her heart. She had progressed through the police by destroying all that stood in her way. Her clean up rate on crime was high, and she cleverly connected with her peers. No one dared to question her authority, and that made her all the more dangerous.

Butler would have a plan, Cornish was sure, and heaven help anyone who got in her way, whether it be professional or personal.

Chapter Five

Cornish parked her beige Volkswagen Camper on the circular driveway of Holland House. She could have done with another eight hours sleep, but that was wishful thinking. After all the drama of the previous evening, she wanted to see the gothic home in all its glory in daylight hours and the murder scene. By the time the body had been collected for transportation to the mortuary, her team had been exhausted. The whole area had been cordoned off, and Cornish had given the rest of her team orders to stay at home for the Sunday. The same rules didn't apply to her. While everything was fresh in her mind, Cornish wanted to refresh her memory of the evening in natural light. DCS Butler wanted an initial report in the morning, and Cornish didn't want to give her any excuse to remove her from the case.

After all the drama of the previous evening, her team would have a bevy of paperwork to go through. And calls to make on Monday. There would be no time off. This was going to be another case to affect the budget for Devon and Cornwall Police.

She doubted that there would be any further allocation of staff to help. Her team would be stretched.

Cornish was surprised by how cold the guests had been at the Halloween Ball and especially the party that Elliot Abbott had been with considering a murder had taken place. He had been a familiar face on the social network of parties and events. And by all accounts was well-liked, according to the others in the Abbott party. Cornish knew there would be more to Elliot Abbott than this first impression, especially given the feedback from the other guests. He was murdered in front of his so-called friends, and it was apparent someone didn't like him. Cornish had taken the decision to go through the dead man's life with a fine-tooth comb. She intended to ruffle a few feathers.

Cornish embraced the solitude as she wandered around Holland House. There were no outside security cameras other than at the front and back entrance. Cornish doubted the murderer would have used one of them. There was a door from the basement to the outside that was obscured. That would have been the obvious choice. Inside, there were cameras throughout the rooms monitoring the staff and guests. Cornish wanted to look at those. But according to Callum Roberts, there were no back-ups from that night. They had been switched off.

The staff count given by Callum Roberts was also somewhat hazy given his meticulous flair for detail and protecting his guests. Cornish wondered what Callum Roberts was hiding. Surely he would need an accurate log of who was working shifts to be able to pay his staff. The thought occurred to Cornish that Roberts was an accomplice if he had knowingly helped the murderer have access to the event.

Cornish glanced through the staff present during the evening. It was a long list of some thirty workers, and yet when they had questioned them last night, they could only account for twenty. Callum Roberts had claimed the other team had left early and he may have made a mistake with the final numbers. Cornish didn't believe in coincidences and doubted staff would have gone early considering the generous tips that would be dispersed at the end of an evening such as this one. There could only be one other conclusion. Callum Roberts was skimming off the top by claiming more staff were working. Cornish made a note to have all the staff and wages checked and Callum Roberts' bank accounts.

Cornish looked at the elite list of guests. As she was scanning through the names, her mobile phone came to life. She was caught off guard initially assuming it was Jamie. She recognised that the caller was Chief Constable Jane Falconbridge.

The two women got on well. If Jane Falconbridge had had her way, Cornish would be the new DCS instead of Danielle Butler. But, Cornish had turned down the vacant position, and CC Jane Falconbridge had been left with no choice, much as it had pained her to do, but to offer the job to Butler.

CC Jane Falconbridge wanted an update on the murder last night. Her tone was warm and friendly, unlike DCS Butler, whose manner was clipped and cold. Cornish briefed her Chief Constable before Falconbridge rang off to answer another call. Cornish slipped her mobile back into her pocket and carried on unaware that she was closely watched by Callum Roberts. When she eventually spotted him, she raised her hand to acknowledge his presence. Cornish was about to call him over when her mobile phone rang. It was the devil herself on the line.

Chapter Six

Cornish was caught off her guard by the call from DCS Butler. Danielle Butler wanted an update and was somewhat irritated that Cornish had spoken to CC Jane Falconbridge before her. Cornish didn't bother to explain that her Chief Constable had contacted her, and not the other way around. That would only serve to annoy her boss, DCS Butler, further. She would consider herself overlooked and not in charge. Danielle Butler had many flaws, and insecurity was one of them.

Danielle Butler was fully aware of Cornish's feelings towards her. There was no love lost between the pair. As far as Butler was concerned, she had been the reserve candidate for the Detective Chief Superintendent position. But she was now the boss, duly appointed by Chief Constable Falconbridge, and Cornish had lost. Failure to accept the position offered meant Cornish was now her lackey and at her beck and call. It irked her that Cornish and Jane Falconbridge were still on such friendly terms.

DCS Butler schooled her features into a professional mask, even on the telephone. Keeping the pretence up at all times was essential. It would be disastrous if Cornish were to read her innermost thoughts and desires she harboured only in private. Work and her career were her passion, and she intended to shine in her new role before she took her plan to the next level. Cornish had no idea what Butler was up to, and Danielle Butler smiled as she considered her next move. She would take great delight in destroying Cornish's career and private life, and in that order.

Cornish stood outside the main entrance to Holland House irritated by the call from Butler when she spotted Callum Roberts getting into his car. She walked towards him, noting his nervous disposition, rather like a naughty child that had been caught out. He shifted uncomfortably in his seat, barely glancing in her direction. DCI Cornish was used to making people feel uncomfortable as she leaned towards Callum Roberts through his open window, smiling. His high-handedness might work with his staff, but faced with Cornish, Callum Roberts demeanour changed, and he twitched and licked his lips. He was decidedly uncomfortable. Callum Roberts was guilty of something. Fiddling the accounts most likely. Cornish filed that little nugget away.

'Morning Mr Roberts. Did you manage to get much sleep? Any thoughts on who would want to murder Elliot Abbott? You seemed to know the guests well.'

Callum Roberts looked across at Cornish and with an obsequious smile he spoke.

'Hell of a night last night,' he remarked with a long sad-faced expression.

'We are all still in shock. Can't quite believe it really happened.'

'Murder can do that, Mr Roberts. I will need to address all the staff again tomorrow, including those who were on the list but left early, if you don't mind. Please make sure they are all here in the morning at 10 am sharp.'

Cornish turned on her heels and retraced her steps back to her VW before giving Callum Roberts the chance to reply. Callum Roberts was a worried man. If his employer found out what he had been up to over the years, then he would be a dead man. He wiped the sweat from his brow and watched Cornish in his rear-view mirror drive away.

Three Months Earlier

Chapter Seven

Glan Morgan stood at the desk, picking up his stuff. It wasn't much, a few hundred pounds. That was what his life was currently worth. He walked out of HMP Exeter, having served the minimum sentence of three years. As he left another prisoner was just signing his release papers, and he and Glan Morgan acknowledged each other. His name was James Foy, and he had spent most of his life in and out of prison. His last sentence had been for murder. As they walked out together, a photographer took their picture. Neither man noticed.

Glan Morgan had been caught with an extraordinary amount of crack cocaine for his own addiction and to supply. At first, he had only sold to friends, but then he expanded to fund his own habit. Glan Morgan made more than he earned as a stockbroker in the beating heart of the City of London. He had a great run for a while, made a shitload of money and then everything that could go wrong did. Morgan messed up royally. He had been living well beyond his means, and he thought dealing drugs would get him out of the hole.

He was a natural salesman or a con artist. It depended on your view. He sailed close to the wind on every deal he ever made, and his friends and colleagues felt sorry for his wife and family. But everyone that knew him liked him for some reason. He was an easy bloke to like.

Glan Morgan hadn't wanted to join the family business, Crown Carpets. They made and supplied carpets to Her Majesty, The Queen. They were the proud recipient of the Royal Warrant of Appointment recognition. He wanted more from life than mere carpets.

Glan wanted to make it on his own. Except that he couldn't help himself to not take or borrow from others. It was part of his make-up. He had sticky fingers. He dabbled in stolen goods, and his life was a constant struggle until he found his niche on the

London Stock Exchange. That world was a giant pot of money for the taking, and for the briefest of time, Glan was the golden boy. He always had a scheme and an agenda. He made money, lots of it, and life for a short while was terrific. He met and married Marie, and they had three children in quick succession.

They bought a London townhouse, and it looked like the road ahead would be smooth finally, when for no reason anyone could fathom, things started to go wrong. The tide had turned, the pressure and hours took their toll, and he turned to drugs to cope. That was his downfall. He started cutting corners, his grand plans and shaky deals, taking him further down the wrong path. He couldn't escape and was in big trouble.

With his drug habit out of control, he was haemorrhaging money and the company he worked for asked him to leave. The only asset left was the London townhouse, and Marie wanted to move back home to Cornwall to be near both families. And she wanted a divorce. Glan had no choice but to borrow money to not only fund his drug habit but to clear off the debt owed. The London house sold would allow him to buy Marie and the children a substantial home and clear his debts leaving enough for a deposit on his own place. Glan was confident he could make up the shortfall quickly and recover his fortune. He was wrong.

Glan's parents distanced themselves. They were ashamed of their only son. They sided with Marie and their three grandchildren. Glan Morgan, who was always used to being in control, no longer called the shots. He always had a plan, and if he had stayed on the right side of the law, then he would have gone far. Glan had been well educated, gone to the best schools and was a genius with money, or so it seemed. He had the world at his feet and everything it took to make his life a success, along with the perfect family. All the trappings weren't enough, though, he wanted more and quickly. But there is no such thing as a free lunch, and Glan was about to pay a hefty price. He couldn't pay back the borrowed money and discreetly embezzled money from the family business. The family covered up his debts and the potential embarrassment. Still, Marie refused to allow him to see his children until he had sorted himself out. Glan Morgan spiralled out of control. He couldn't stop his drug habit, and he borrowed more money to support his lifestyle while losing money on high-risk investments. Glan Morgan was in debt for a fortune and hadn't seen his children for a year when he was finally arrested for the drugs-related crime of possession and dealing. He didn't have the money to pay anyone back and assumed a spell in prison would cancel out any debts unpaid. He was wrong.

Chapter Eight

Glan Morgan was broke. Double-crossed and in debt for a fortune. He had paid no one back for three years while inside. The dealers wanted their money back, and although he'd paid the price in prison time, now he was out, and they were after him again for their money.

Glan hadn't seen his children and was unlikely to see them anytime soon. Yet he wanted to live near his family, in Cornwall. He wanted to make up for the lost years and try to reconnect on some level. But, every time he drove past the house, which should have been his home, he thought about all the money he had lost, and how he had been double-crossed and let down on so many levels, this hatred rose up from nowhere. He had been replaced by an estate agent of all people. The very person who had sold Marie the house was now living in the home he had paid for and bringing up his children. Glan wanted him dead.

Glan Morgan now lived in a small flat in St Austell with no family or life to return to. His parents had made it perfectly clear that he wasn't welcome until he had sorted his life out. His future was looking bleak, and he had no desire to return to prison. He was drug-free, flat broke but healthy and still incredibly good-looking. Something good was going to happen to him eventually. At forty, Glan Morgan still had time to turn his life full circle. Hopefully, the mistakes of the past had taught him a lesson.

Glan Morgan had a probation officer, and a list of rules he had to abide by under his licence conditions. He had every intention of keeping clean from drugs and trouble-free. He wanted to see his children again and rebuild his relationships. He wanted his life back.

The joy of getting released was to be short-lived.

Chapter Nine

Rebecca Keane sat staring at the photos on her kitchen table. She felt she had been staring at the same pictures for months. Her husband looked incredibly handsome in the photographs, and the woman with him was smiling. It should have been her in the picture, not this two-timing bitch. She had taken her revenge by having her own affair. Her husband never even noticed. All Becky wanted was to be married to the man she had first fallen in love with.

Becky blamed the house. She now knew it was a bad omen the moment they walked into 13 Falmouth Road. That's when their problems started, coupled with the fact that her husband, the famous Jason Keane, could no longer play professional football. His career was in tatters due to a persistent back injury, and he was facing retirement.

Jason Keane had been at the top of his game when they met. He had swept Becky off her feet, and within twelve months they were married, and their wedding was photographed for Hello Magazine. They decided to live in Cornwall as Becky wanted to be near her family and they brought their first house in Falmouth Road, No 13. It was more than Becky had ever dreamed of, hoped for, needed, or wanted, initially.

Suddenly they were in this world of celebrity status, Jason had the stellar career and everything he claimed he had always wanted. Their two girls went to the private school in Truro and Becky insisted she took care of her children. Becky had no marketable skills; all she knew how to be was a wife and mother. And then Jason's career was over.

The life of glamour and fame that Becky and Jason had craved was gone, for good. Yes, they had famous friends, yes, they were invited to all the parties. But no, they could never hope to compete financially anymore with their so-called celebrity friends. They still had money, more than most people, but nothing compared to their friends.

They had enough money in the bank for Jason to retire and for them to live comfortably in Cornwall. But, neither wanted to give up their lifestyle and compromise with the decline of Jason's health.

Jason was then offered a chance of doubling his money. He joined forces with their close-knit group of friends to form a consortium. Together they started building up a portfolio of companies, that on paper they had yet to prove successful. For the first three years, every business they touched turned to gold. Their fortunes doubled as predicted.

The opportunity then came up to purchase Tresco House in Feock, and they took it. Becky loved the palatial house, and it would be a fresh start for the whole family.

13 Falmouth Road was not an easy house to sell. They purchased Tresco thinking Falmouth Road would sell quickly, but every prospective sale fell through. The house was in one of the best

roads in Truro and arguably one of the best homes, yet 13 Falmouth Road would not budge.

The wave continued for Jason as they invested in high-risk companies. Then came the scandal involving one of the companies which unbeknown to Jason they had invested in as a silent partner. No one knew officially who was involved, and the losses were concealed from the press and the media. Within six months, almost everything had gone, and Jason was licking his wounds. They desperately needed a sale on 13 Falmouth Road. Jason was beginning to feel surrounded by the stench of failure, first his health and now this. His entire ego had been wrapped up in his fortune. He felt guilty for having had an affair, and he wanted to make things right like before. They were near to ruin if they didn't sell 13 Falmouth Road. He had just turned forty and the success that had meant everything to him for the last few years was suddenly over. And nothing Becky said seemed to console him. The only money they had left was in the two houses. To the average man on the street that would be more than adequate but to the likes of Jason Keane, a once-famous footballer, it was simply not good enough.

Then out of the blue, they had another viewing for 13 Falmouth Road. Abbott & Abbott were marketing the property. Becky made sure the house was immaculate, and the inspection went ahead. Maxwell Abbott, with all his charm, showed the client around and before the day was over, they had an offer which they accepted for a quick sale. It looked as if their luck was finally turning. The conveyancing commenced, and everything appeared to be going well. The buyer was keen to move in as soon as possible and wanted a further visit to 13 Falmouth Road. This time Elliot Abbott was there to greet her.

And that's when things started to go wrong.

Chapter Ten

Ashley Roberts had been assured by her ex-husband that everything was going to turn around again very quickly and not to worry. Her divorce settlement would be paid very soon. She could move out of the family home. He would take that burden on, and Ashley could move on with her life. That was when she saw 13 Falmouth Road. Ashley had loved Truro from the very start and wanted to live in the city. This was her dream home. Everything she had ever wanted. Her offer was accepted, and she made plans, grand plans. And then everything fell apart.

Ashley Roberts couldn't continue with the purchase of 13 Falmouth Road. She had paid the exchange money and failed to complete. Jason and Becky Keane had no idea why. Abbott & Abbott tried to contact her but failed miserably. Her solicitor would make no comment other than the fact that his client had changed her mind for reasons he couldn't fathom. The only silver lining for Jason and Becky was the deposit money, which they kept. And once again, 13 Falmouth Road was back on the market.

The deal in Russia didn't happen. There was suddenly another catastrophe in her ex-husband's financial life. It had been like this since their divorce eight years earlier. He made deal after deal and always told her the same thing. He would recoup all their losses and pay back the money he had taken, stolen, from the family home and their bank accounts and Ashley. With all the accounts drained, Ashley Roberts was ruined. Her dream house had evaporated.

For her ex-husband, he had one last shot of victory. He had spent the last few years climbing Everest and falling off again with one defeat after the next. He was closer to sixty than forty and if his fortunes didn't turn around soon then life as he knew it would soon be over. He refused to recognise his failure. If he admitted it was over, then there would be little point in continuing with life. He couldn't live on fresh air alone. And he didn't want to live just an ordinary life. He wanted more than that. Much more.

Nothing mattered to Ashley anymore. She sat in her home and sobbed telling herself that life wasn't worth living. She felt like she'd be a laughingstock around the world, or at least her small world of Cornwall. Ashley Roberts was a fighter, but she couldn't see a way to dig herself out of this hole. On the verge of losing her home through her ex-husband leveraging their assets, and continuously borrowing more, it would be only a matter of time. The debts she was facing were overwhelming if her home didn't sell. She was selling everything that wasn't nailed down. The truth was that Ashley barely had enough money, and she couldn't wait to sell the house. Yet she refused to believe her life was over. Ashley wouldn't declare herself bankrupt. While she couldn't get a job that would pay enough to sustain the bills in her large family home, she could sell some of her jewellery to keep the bank away for a while longer. And now she was angry because she had lost the exchange deposit money on 13 Falmouth Road. Ashley had to admit to her solicitor that her ex-husband had reneged on the divorce settlement. He wasn't surprised.

Ashley felt totally isolated by all that had happened. She had lived in her home for seventeen years. The children had grown up there and loved it, but there was nothing Ashley could do about it now. She was still trying to keep the extent of their financial disaster a secret to avoid worrying them. They were grown up and had homes of their own, yet they still considered this their main home.

Worse yet, 13 Falmouth Road and her last visit there had opened up old wounds. She'd rather be dead than face 'him' again and the horror and shame of the world finding out. The memories had come flooding back of that night, decades ago and the subsequent occasions. It had taken Ashley years to come to terms with her past, and many hours in therapy. In one swoop, the past had all come rushing back. The dreams had restarted, and they always ended the same way, with a death. But Ashley never knew who died, the faces changed. Sometimes it was her, sometimes it was him and his best friend back then, and other times it was a random stranger.

Meeting Elliot Abbott had changed everything. For years Ashley had managed to function in the real world putting aside the nightmare of what happened. Still, on seeing Elliot Abbott for the first time since childhood, she couldn't let it go anymore.

Ashley hadn't seen Elliot since he was a teenager. She had been five years old at the time. He and a friend had been babysitting her and her baby brother while her parents were out. And that had been the start of the abuse and the nightmare.

They say you never forget your attacker. Ashley Roberts had never in a million years expected to see Elliot Abbott again. But as soon as he introduced himself, she instantly recognised him. He was nearly sixty, but she knew it was him. The eyes and the same mannerisms, and he still retained an element of sleaziness. Ashley suspected he was just the same and wondered how many others he had harmed during his life. She had spent hours since that meeting looking at her old photographs. He had been a family friend's son and visited her parent's home on many occasions. It was a tangle of horror and lies that haunted Ashley, day and night. At the same time, she wrestled with the loss of any financial safety net and this latest discovery.

Elliot Abbott was back in her life.

Chapter Eleven

Elliot Abbott hadn't recognised Ashley. Not at first. It was the letter, received, that alerted him. Now everything made sense. Ashley Roberts was all grown up and had gotten herself a set of balls.

Elliot recalled the first time he and Eric had entered her bedroom. They had been watching porn for weeks, and neither one had a girlfriend. This tiny blonde-haired child lay asleep upstairs, and they crept into her bedroom. The child was in a double bed. The two young men walked up to her and started stroking her hair. Ashley stirred and wiped her eyes, wondering who was there. She didn't look scared when she saw them, they were meant to be her friends. They talked gently at first and then Elliot opened his trousers. He was fully aroused as he made Ashley hold him, and he gently rubbed himself with her hand. Eric, in the meantime, stood there watching, masturbating. Elliot then reached down and touched Ashley, fondling her sex. She felt like velvet, soft and small. Both young men relieved themselves on her stomach that night before cleaning Ashley up and leaving her to cry herself to sleep. Elliot told her it would be their little secret and she mustn't say anything to her parents. Otherwise, they would hurt her. How many times did they visit her bedroom after that? He knew the answer.

Elliot realised he had an erection. After all these years little Ashley Roberts still got him excited. Her letter had been perfunctory, reminding him of his crimes. Perhaps Ashley Roberts had missed their visits. She was right about one thing. He hadn't changed. He had always been careful and worked alone and online. His position allowed him the odd liaison with a desperate housewife or two. At the same time, their rich husbands played golf or fucked the mistress, but it was the really young ones he craved. He had sailed too close to home last time with Becky Keane, and he wouldn't make that mistake again. She had two beautiful young girls to protect, and when she realised what Elliot Abbott really wanted, she broke it off. If Jason had known he would have killed Elliot.

Elliot Abbott had met and married Marie, his second wife, a few years earlier when she purchased a townhouse from him. His first wife, Annette, had discovered his dirty little secret and divorced him on the quiet to avoid any embarrassment in their shared social circle. They had no children, but Marie came with three, two girls and a boy, and Elliot struggled to keep his deep perverted affection for the children under control.

Eric went back to his native France after university, and the two pals had lost touch. Elliot took one last look at the letter before disregarding it and placing it back in his jacket pocket. A memento of the past. He would burn it later. It would be her word against his if she reported it to the police, which he doubted. Nobody would believe her.

Elliot Abbott had more important things to worry about. The papers had talked about the demise of various companies in the recent market. Miraculously nobody had strung the entire picture together and joined the dots. That would have been disastrous if others had guessed the principle investors. It was already bad enough. Elliot and Jason's old partner, Charles Rapier, had known they had invested his money and lost it all. Now, Charles Rapier wanted what was rightfully his back.

Chapter Twelve

Ashley refused to resort to medication. She would see this through to the bitter end if necessary. Miraculously Ashley suddenly had three buyers after her home. Utterly broken and in despair, she emptied her house of all her possessions and managed to place them in three containers. Her whole life in three large boxes. The rest sold off for nothing. When all was said and done, she only had herself to think about now and the cat. She needed a roof over her head and a job. It didn't matter anymore. Very little did.

During the day, Ashley put on a brave face. It was the night times that overwhelmed her with waves of panic about her future. Nothing good had come from the divorce her way, and she was still thinking about what the future held. No one spoke to her about her situation. People didn't know what to say. It was almost as though the loss would be contagious. Women with safe, comfortable, normal lives and husbands didn't want to get too near her. She was suddenly single and alone for the first time since her divorce, and she felt like a pariah.

Ashley was worried about what she was going to live on. She had paid all the debts owing. Having gone from rags to riches to rags again, her story was more extreme than most. She had her survival to think about. She had no desire to meet anyone else, in fact, quite the reverse. One marriage had been more than enough, And, she had said as much to her children. Her ex-husband had let them all down, Ashley's future and her children's inheritance. Ashley now had to think for herself and make her own future.

With the sale of her home progressing to completion, Ashley was busy trying to sort out where she was going to live. Her options were limited, and she was hoping for something to turn up. She didn't want to burden the children with her problems. As she stood looking around at the bare walls and empty rooms where her family had lived for seventeen years, it was like seeing the last of her dreams disappear.

The chalet at Gwithian Sands was empty, and if Ashley was prepared to help tidy it up and decorate it, then she could stay there. Ashley was grateful for a roof over her head. It was the ideal place for her to plan her next move.

Ashley could see no way forward without putting the past behind her, and the only way she could do that would be to rid the world of the likes of Elliot Abbott.

Chapter Thirteen

Eight weeks earlier, Marie Abbott had been a happily married woman with a loving husband who adored her three children. She thought they had no money worries, they were all in good health, and nothing terrible would happen to them. Eight weeks later, Marie Abbott wanted a divorce. Except it would be 'over his dead body,' as Elliot Abbott had put it during their argument. It was almost too much to believe.

There was nothing wrong with their marriage from Elliot's perspective, and even Marie admitted that she'd been happy with him. That was until the visit from Ashley Roberts. Elliot was now seething. That explained the sudden change of Marie's heart and the current state of his marriage.

Marie Abbott had never suspected a thing, and it hadn't happened immediately. She had fallen in love with Elliot at a time in her life when she was vulnerable. He had been a great support during her divorce and wonderfully supportive and sympathetic and kind to her. He had found her a beautiful home, and then they had dinner one night, just casually, and it had taken off from there. They got married, and everything seemed perfect. Elliot loved her and her children. Sometimes Marie thought he loved them more than her.

Everything now made sense. Elliot's over attentiveness with her children, the late-night cuddles. How could she have missed the signs? Her mind ran away with all the possibilities once she knew what he was. She had searched through their computer and found images that would scar her for life. She felt physically sick when she considered the danger she had placed her children in. At least she knew why Annette had left him now.

Marie told Elliot she wanted a divorce and to sell the house. She didn't want anything associated with him. It wouldn't have helped Elliot to say to her that he had never actually touched her children. Marie wouldn't have believed him.

Elliot wanted half of the money out of the house sale. He needed that money after his business losses. If Marie wanted a divorce, then it was going to cost her. He would miss her and miss the children.

Marie Abbott stood staring at their bedroom wall, as she thought of the argument she'd had with him. She had never felt so lost and alone in her life. Everything she thought she had believed in and counted on, and thought would always be there for her, no longer was. And the worst thing was that she hadn't done anything wrong, at least she didn't think she had. She had been the perfect loving wife and made Elliot's life comfortable, and she had never once complained. Just thinking about it all made her feel sick.

Ashley Roberts had wrecked Elliot's marriage, and she would pay. He drove back to the office and pretended everything was normal while he tried to think about what to do. He didn't want to lose the home that Marie had bought, and she wasn't shifting on selling and giving him a penny.

Elliot did his thinking at night, when it all came back to him again, his past. He thought about the children he had hurt, again and again, and how much they had cried.

Elliot Abbott was going nowhere.

Chapter Fourteen

Glan Morgan should have been an antique dealer. He had all the attributes necessary for that trade: devious, less than scrupulous and with the gift of the gab. A people watcher extraordinaire. He just wanted to taste his freedom. When he heard that Marie had remarried an Estate Agent, of all things, it grated him. But, Glan had more important things to sort out, such as what he intended to do now for a living. For the moment, he had no idea.

Glan Morgan called every contact he'd ever had for a job. Any job to get him back on his feet and keep him close to his family. People had moved, faces had changed, and those that remembered him ignored or refused to take his calls. Everyone knew he had gone to prison, and no one was keen to help him, let alone see him. He was officially persona non grata. His history was too checkered, too dodgy. Glan was prepared to do anything, work in a restaurant, a supermarket, you name it, but by the end of three weeks, he was no further to finding a job. He was beginning to feel desperate, and then he received the one phone call he had been dreading.

Charles Rapier owned a high-tech stock listed public company along with other businesses he preferred the taxman to know little about. And, Glan Morgan owed him money, a lot of money. He had worked for Charles Rapier, made him wealthier, and himself in the process. When Glan announced he was setting up on his own, Charles Rapier double-crossed him. And now he was caught between a rock and a hard place. Glan hated Charles Rapier and blamed him for his bad luck and life of crime. He'd spent his time in prison thinking about taking his revenge and then on his release thinking about ways to avoid bumping into Rapier again. It was inevitable their paths would cross. Glan Morgan couldn't help but be attracted back to the opportunity of making large amounts of money, and fast, even though it was against his licence conditions. If he wanted his family back again, he had little choice.

Glan recognised the number as he answered his mobile. And two hours later he was sitting in Charles Rapier's Cornish retreat.

'Well, this is a surprise,' Rapier said in an unpleasant tone.

'How long have you been out?'

Rapier already knew the answer but wanted to watch Glan Morgan squirm.

'About three weeks,' Glan said quietly.

There was no question in Rapier's mind that he was Glan Morgan's only option and way out of his current predicament. He had seen to that by closing every door. He had Glan Morgan by the balls, and Morgan knew it. Glan had no choice.

'I have a job for you,' Rapier said bluntly. This will clear your debt to me. Glan Morgan was perfect for what Rapier had in mind.

Charles Rapier was rotten. He had a beautiful wife, and three children but to those that knew him well, they knew he wore many masks. To the rest of the world, he seemed successful, charming, a family man and well respected. Glan Morgan knew better.

Rapier had just the job for Morgan. Rather than have him killed in prison or made somebody's bitch he made sure Morgan remained safe inside. Rapier knew Morgan would be useful to him one day, and desperate when he came out. Rapier was offering Morgan a piece of the pie, his debts written off and a share of the gains if he carried out his plan. This was the opportunity Glan Morgan had been waiting for. Glan was grateful until he heard the project.

'You may need to hire someone, that's up to you. But I am to be consulted and kept up to date,' replied Rapier.

With that, he handed Glan the file. In it were clippings and reports on virtually everything Jason Keane had undertaken for the last fifteen years since leaving professional football. All his businesses and investments, and the other partners involved.

Jason Keane had quietly amassed a significant fortune. Rapier had at one time been part of the consortium, but because of his lack of popularity he had been ousted, and that had seriously pissed him off. He had lost a fortune on investments he should have received a share of. Ostracised both financially and personally, Rapier now wanted revenge. The final insult was at Holland House when he went unrecognised. Rapier wanted his money.

Rapier replaced the file on Jason Keane and smiled across the desk at Glan again.

'I want you to kidnap his children, and in return, we are going to ask for the sum of twenty million pounds.'

Glan Morgan stared speechless as Rapier continued. He was insane if he thought Gan would assist in kidnapping and blackmail. Rapier had planned the entire scenario. Morgan would kidnap the two little girls, hold on to them until the money was paid, and then release them.

'I won't do it. Find someone else to do your dirty work for you,'
as Glan stood up and started to walk away.

'I wouldn't do that if I were you,' Rapier said with an evil smile.
I believe you have three children of your own?'

Glan looked suddenly worried. Rapier's eyes never left Glan's
face and
Glan felt something icy cold and terrifying run down his spine,
fear. Rapier wasn't joking. If Glan didn't do what he wanted then
his children would die. Glan could deal with the whole kidnap
plan himself or get help. Either way, Rapier would pay him five
million pounds to run the show. The ground rules were clear.
Kidnap Jason Keane's children or else his children were dead.

Rapier was clearly deranged, and Glan Morgan wanted nothing to
do with his plan. And Glan wanted none of these children to get
hurt. Suddenly there were five lives at stake. Rapier handed Glan
one hundred thousand pounds upfront. He had him firmly by the

balls. If he warned Marie, their children would be killed. If he warned Jason Keane, his children would be killed. If he alerted the police, his children would be killed. There was no way he was going to risk losing his children. He was a dead man either way. If he got caught, he would spend the rest of his life in prison. Rapier had him over a barrel.

'What if Keane hasn't got the money?' Glan asked.

'The man's loaded. This will be pocket money to him. Let me know when you plan to kidnap them,' and with that Glan, was dismissed. As he walked outside, he got into his clapped-out car and drove out of Rapier's estate. He pulled into the nearest layby, opened the driver's door and threw up.

Chapter Fifteen

Glan Morgan couldn't carry out the kidnapping without help.
That help would come at a cost. He needed someone capable of
carrying out such a crime. He was still feeling sick about it. His
life was over, and he almost wished he was still back in prison.
At least there, life was simple. All hope of having a decent life
after his release was now looking hopeless. It was over for him
whatever he did. He had to start thinking smart and who he was
going to hire for Rapier's pet project. It was going to be difficult
to find someone to trust with such a delicate matter, and he felt
sick in the pit of his stomach just thinking about it. He only had
one man in mind who could be capable of kidnapping, James
Foy. He knew he was in Cornwall. Foy had mentioned something
along the lines when they walked out of HMP Exeter Prison
together. All Glan had to do was locate him.

Glan Morgan purchased a burner mobile as instructed by Rapier
and left Rapier his contact details. From the little conversation
he'd had with James Foy, Glan knew Foy had grown up in

Holmbush, just outside St Austell. The first place to enquire would be the local pub. Any prisoner worth his salt on release would grab a pint. The Holmbush Inn was the obvious choice. Glan Morgan walked into the pub during lunchtime and came face to face with Foy. Walking towards the bar, Foy recognised Morgan and signalled to a table in the corner. Foy didn't want the locals to overhear any conversation. No one knew where he had been the past years, and he wanted it to stay that way. Old buddies didn't yet know he had been released and he wasn't keen to rekindle old acquaintances.

If Foy was surprised to see Morgan, he didn't show it. Instead, he brought two pints over and sat down. They didn't know each other but had always been distantly respectful of each other. They had never been associates inside. Foy smiled. It was a relief to see a friendly face.

'What are you doing here?'

Glan Morgan looked suddenly nervous, but he had no choice. He couldn't save the lives of his children without the likes of James Foy. He needed him more than Foy needed him. If he didn't kidnap the Keane children, then his own would be dead. Morgan's voice cracked as he spoke. He had a deadline and a target date. With an envelope of cash in his pocket, he now faced Foy. There was a good chance that the offer Morgan wanted to make Foy would infuriate him, and he might beat the hell out of Morgan for even asking. Glan Morgan wasn't looking forward to broaching it with him.

This was much harder than Glan thought, and a lot scarier. He was asking Foy to get involved in some nasty shit. But there was also a lot of money on the table. It was hard to predict how Foy would react, or what he'd say.

Foy sensed quickly that whatever Glan Morgan had to say was important. The two men hadn't exchanged more than ten words in prison, and now he'd turned up in Holmbush to find him. Foy was curious. He would listen to him, but that was all he was going to do. Waiting, Glan hesitated for a moment and then spoke. There was no avoiding it if Glan wanted his help.

'Someone has offered me a business deal,' Glan started to say as Foy listened. 'I don't know if you'd be interested, but I wanted to talk to you. I owe this person a lot of money, and my ass is on the line, and my family's. I have no choice, but I can't do this on my own, at least not easily. If I don't do this for him now, he says he'll kill my children. I believe him.'

'He sounds a nice person. What's the job?' Foy's voice was non-committal.

'There's a lot of money on the table, one million pounds to you if you're in.'

Foy whistled at the amount.

'How much do you get?'

'Four million. He wants me to get the right men for the job. I thought of you. And maybe one other. He wants us to kidnap someone and hold them until the ransom is paid and then send them home, alive. With luck, this will be over quickly, and no one will get hurt.'

'Who the fuck are we to kidnap?' Foy asked.

'Two girls. The parents will pay for their safe return.'
Now saying it out loud Glan wasn't convinced. The plan had sounded better in his head. Now it sounded absurd.

Foy leaned across the table and leered at Morgan.
'If you are fucking with me, I'll kill you and your kids myself, do you understand?'
'Are you in? And have you got someone else who can help? He'll be paid the same.' Glan needed an answer. Time was of the essence.

James Foy looked straight at Glan Morgan and nodded. He had someone in mind, and it would be his deal with the other person.

Morgan agreed and went over the rest of the plan. Foy had a job which he couldn't get out of so easily without it looking suspicious. Thus, Morgan would carry out the necessary surveillance for the next few weeks, and Foy would get his mate to take over surveillance at the weekends. It wouldn't be easy since the family lived in Penpol. A stranger would look out of place there. Glan Morgan had thought of that.

James Foy trusted Glan Morgan, he didn't say that, but he also thought he was naïve. This was a big deal, and if anybody talked, they would all be screwed and back behind bars.

'Presumably, the ransom will be paid quickly.' Foy didn't want to have to kill two children.

Foy stood up then and looked at Glan, still sitting. He'd heard enough, and he needed to think about it.

'I'll let you know. How do I get hold of you?'

Glan handed him his burner mobile number written down already on a piece of paper. It wasn't the kind of decision anyone could make instantly. Glan was asking a lot.

Two days later, Glan Morgan's mobile rang. At first, he thought it was Rapier and was relieved when Foy spoke.

'We're in.'

Chapter Sixteen

Glan Morgan watched as Becky Keane drove away from Tresco House. Even at forty, Becky was spectacular looking with her long blonde hair. She had features like a cameo and a lovely figure. The severe troubled look in her eyes made her look older than her years.

The husband, Jason Keane, left for work roughly the same time each day. He drove the family sports car, a Bentley, while Becky Keane drove the family, Range Rover.

Morgan reported back to Rapier daily. He sounded pleased with their progress. Morgan had organised transport for them all and rented a place in Point, under an assumed name, a few minutes' walk from the Keane's residence. He didn't want to stand out as a total stranger and blending in seemed a much better option. The detached small house was fairly isolated on the outskirts of the village. Morgan could walk around unnoticed taking in the road up to Tresco House without anybody thinking it was odd. He bumped into Becky and the children in the local store a couple of times and smiled at the girls. When Morgan wasn't watching the family, James Foy and his friend took over. Morgan had yet to meet the third man. He didn't know anything about him and preferred to keep it that way.

Glan Morgan watched Becky Keane drop off her children at the private school in Truro and then, more often than not, she would go back home and work out in their home gym and swimming pool. Then she would leave the house dressed up and eat lunch somewhere, with a girlfriend, before collecting the children from school. She didn't work. Jason Keane would be home in time to see his two girls and have a family dinner, and they entertained a lot. Glan Morgan was convinced by the end of the first two weeks that they had the money.

The weekly dinner parties were lively, the guests well known, even Glan Morgan recognised them. He was surprised by their set of celebrity friends, and the more he watched the family, the more convinced he was of their wealth.

It was James Foy who brought him back down to earth with a reality check. They were here to kidnap the two little girls. Who was going to get hold of the guns? Glan Morgan hadn't thought that far ahead and hadn't considered they would need them. But, as Foy pointed out, they weren't playing nice, and this was a severe crime that could turn nasty any moment. Foy still had his contacts, and he would handle the artillery.

Glan didn't like the sound of it, but he had no choice. As Glan hung up, he had the now-familiar pain in his stomach. He was beginning to think it was his conscience. Following Becky Keane around, and then seeing his own children from a distance was making him nervous about the whole thing. Glan didn't know just what James Foy was capable of and he had, as yet, to meet the third man. He had caught a glimpse of him a couple of times as he took over the surveillance, but he didn't have a clue to the man's character. Had he known that Miles Fisher had no scruples, he would have been an even more worried man.

Miles Fisher had, like James Foy, been brought up in prison. He had served his apprenticeship inside and what he didn't know about prison life wasn't worth knowing. He was a survivor, a killer from animals to children to adults and the elderly. Handing Miles Fisher a gun would be a mistake. Miles Fisher was the wild card in the deck.

The surveillance was almost over, and the date had been set. They could get on with it. Foy and Fisher were keen to get their hands on the money and disappear.

All had gone to plan so far, and Glan Morgan hoped the next part would have no glitches. He had already taken too many risks. He had forgotten to inform his parole officer that he had moved, and this would definitely constitute breaking his probation rules.

Monday 5 November

Chapter Seventeen

Bleary-eyed Cornish emerged from her bed, alone, to shower, dress and prepare for the long week ahead. She was looking forward to the particular circumstances of their living environment changing.

Jamie would be in Bristol for the rest of the week. They were increasingly at ease with each other. Claire couldn't quite believe how, in such a short time, she had gone from being comfortably single to missing Jamie in her cosy cottage when he was away. They had slipped into a post-weekend routine which saw Jamie leave early on a Monday morning to get to Bristol for his first meeting of the morning.

After she had eaten, she made her way to the hospital, picking up Pearce en route.

'What do you make of Butler? She's more hands-on than Falconbridge was, I know that much,' asked Pearce, sat in the passenger seat next to Cornish.

'It's too early to tell, but I don't trust her one bit. You only see someone's true colours when they are under pressure,' replied Cornish.

'You sound as if you need a distraction?' Pearce said.

'Other than looking at a corpse,' Cornish replied. 'I can think of better things to do on a Monday morning,' as she concentrated on finding a parking spot at the hospital.

'You can't stop someone committing a crime if they've set their mind to it,' Pearce laughed.

'If I could, I'd be out of a job.'

Gary Gilbert was the senior pathologist back at the mortuary at the Royal Cornwall Hospital in Treliske, Truro. He loved his job, his life. He had been going out with one of his young pathology technicians for several months, and Cornish had to admit Gilbert was a changed man. She had never known him to take a break.

Gilbert smiled as he looked up from his desk as his two favourite detectives sat down. He offered Cornish and Pearce coffee and biscuits. Pearce had drawn the short straw that morning to accompany Cornish to the autopsy.

Elliot Abbott was in Room A on the slab.

Gilbert, wearing his white lab coat that covered just past his knees, drew back the paper sheet over Elliot Abbott to reveal the body. He signalled the assistant who came across, and together they turned the body over. Gilbert wanted to explain the cause of death.

'The knife used to kill your man was a Spring Assisted Stiletto Knife which was found at the scene of the murder still in the victims back. The blade was smooth as you can see from the exhibit here,' as Gilbert displayed the knife, 'and there were no fingerprints to be found on the knife other than the victims. I believe he owned the knife as his name is etched on the Pearl inlay handle. Handmade, relatively easy to purchase, I suspect. With a blade length of 12 cm and a thickness of 3 mm. A rather nice stainless steel piece of craftsmanship. As you can see, there is one fatal stab wound which penetrated the heart, killing the victim instantly. Probably more of a lucky aim than anything else, and the weapon was long and sharp enough to penetrate the victims clothing. The obvious blood loss as he bled out and died there and then. No other remarkable findings on the body. He was a healthy man that died from unfortunate circumstances. His last supper was that evening, as you know, and the time of death at 10.30 pm.'

'The victim didn't kill himself,' said Cornish stating the obvious. 'That would be a first. Impossible at that angle to be self-inflicted. What I can say for certain is that he or she wore gloves and was slightly shorter in stature. The angle of entry was upwards. I see from my notes from Turner that there were plenty of prints around the area, and one suggestion would be to find whose prints are missing.'

Gilbert handed Cornish a copy of his findings. As was customary Pearce lit up his cigarette as they exited the building. The smell of the tar seemed to take away the aroma of death from his nostrils.

With the cause of death determined Cornish wondered who the killer was and why Elliot Abbott had been killed in such a public place. She thought to herself that you never knew what sins remained invisible to the naked eye. There was one thing for sure, Elliot Abbott had certainly upset someone. His death was no accident. Who at the Holland House Ball was capable of hurting anyone? That was the question.

Cornish had delegated the task of going through the guest list and staff on duty that night to Hutchens and Mac. Cornish and Pearce would check out Callum Roberts.

Cornish wanted a closer look at the Elliot Abbott party of eight starting with Elliot Abbott himself. What secrets had Elliot Abbott taken to his grave?

Cornish intended to find out.

Chapter Eighteen

Becky had screened her calls and avoided all Elliot Abbotts calls. She didn't want to talk to him except in social gatherings where she couldn't avoid it. Becky had been dreading facing him at the ball. She had barely said two words to him during the evening, and now she couldn't tell him exactly what she thought of him because he was dead.

Becky hadn't seen a dead body before. It was her first. The sight of all that blood made her feel queasy and lightheaded. Time had stood still before Marie Abbott's screams had filled the room.

In the light of day, Becky now wondered what would come out from the woodwork. Everyone's dirty little secrets would be revealed. The police would examine and pull apart all of their lives to find the killer. If they discovered her affair, however brief with Elliot Abbott, then she would be considered a suspect. If they thought that her husband had known about the relationship, then he too would be a suspect. They were all connected, both personally and financially. Elliot Abbott had got them involved in some extremely dodgy deals verging on insider trading, and they had all suffered heavy financial losses.

Elliot Abbott's death was no accident. Becky mustered confidence she didn't entirely feel. She needed to put on a brave face. The police had yet to come knocking on her door.

Chapter Nineteen

Operation Holland House was well underway.

'At least we know it was murder,' exclaimed Mac.

'Any news on the note found in Elliot Abbott's pocket?' Cornish asked.

Hutchens answered.

'Wishful thinking. There were no discernible prints on the note except the victims.'

'How many guests were wearing gloves that evening?' Cornish asked.

'Including ourselves, thirty guests, Ma'am.'

'You could charm the birds from the trees Pearce,' laughed Cornish.

'Can anyone tell me anything about the guests? And especially the Elliot Abbott party.'

Hutchens shook her head.

'They are all keeping schtum.'

'Well, it's time to rattle a few cages then,' replied Cornish swiftly.

Time had a worrying habit of moving on too fast. Cornish didn't want the guests getting too comfortable.

As Cornish dished out instructions, DCS Butler emerged from her office.

'Any news to report?' Butler asked bluntly.

Cornish didn't miss the fact that Danielle Butler was in charge and wanted the whole team to know.

'Nothing as yet,' replied, Cornish curtly.

Pearce looked away and cleared his throat.

In the silence that followed, fuming with indignation, Butler turned on her heels and walked back to her office.

Cornish and Pearce decided to pay Callum Roberts a visit. He was being unhelpful wasting police time. The morning sunshine had turned overcast as they drove onto the estate in Truro. The area was well maintained, and they soon found the address they were looking for. A wrought-iron gate gave access to a gravel pathway leading to the front door. Knocking on the red door, they heard Callum Roberts approaching. They had just missed him at Holland House and were assured he would be home by now. Answering the door, he was somewhat surprised to see the police. He had hoped to avoid the inevitable.

'Come in,' he murmured. 'I wasn't expecting company.'

Once inside, Cornish and Pearce watched the man switch off the kettle and face them. There was a short silence before Cornish's words began to penetrate.

'I think it's high time you told us what's been going on. Your guest list and staff list don't add up. I personally counted eighty-two settings at the tables, two guests weren't on your list.' Cornish stared at Callum Roberts, waiting for a reply.

Shock frittered over Callum Robert's face, and he took a step back, unconsciously defensive.

'I don't know what you are talking about,' he stuttered.

'I think you do Mr Roberts. Shall we stop playing games and start from the beginning, or would you prefer to do this back at the police station.'

Callum Roberts sat down with his head in his hands, trying to compose himself. It made no difference as he blurted out what he knew. He didn't deny it. He had been cooking the books. No one ever noticed a few extra guests, and staff and he'd never been questioned. He couldn't help himself; he was only human after all. He hadn't meant any harm by it.

Cornish and Pearce said nothing at first. They allowed Callum Roberts to spill the beans on all his fiddles and little operations he had going. From the handyman to the cook, to the grocery bill, you name it, he had a finger in every pie. A light sweat trickled down Callum Roberts back. He had been busted.

Cornish interrupted Callum Roberts train of thought.
'There were two entrances into Holland House. The main front entrance and the back used by staff and for deliveries. The only camera on was at the front. Including ourselves,' Cornish pointed to her and Pearce, 'there were eighty-two guests gathered in the dining room before they dispersed into the other rooms after dinner to dance and chat. Who are the missing guests? I suppose it's too much to hope for any CCTV.'

'You suppose correctly,' Callum Roberts confirmed. I disconnected it deliberately, to protect the privacy of the guests that evening. I can't understand why anybody would murder Elliot Abbott. It doesn't make sense.'

'I want to know why the lights failed and whether it was by accident or design. Did you switch the lights off?' asked Cornish.

Once again, Callum Roberts looked sheepishly at the detectives. 'I'm afraid I did. You see there was a note left on my desk requesting that the lights be switched off at a certain time, 10.30 pm. I naturally assumed it was for a surprise of some sorts. I've done that kind of thing before for guests. I didn't think to find out who had left the note there. I wasn't expecting someone to be actually murdered.'

There was a short silence while Callum Roberts digested the enormity of what he had done.

Twenty minutes later, Cornish and Pearce had the names of the two missing guests.

Callum Roberts watched the two officers leave and smiled as he looked in the mirror.

'Callum boy, you should have been an actor.'

He'd told the police enough. He knew exactly who had killed Elliot Abbott. The money he was demanding in exchange for the evidence would be sufficient to keep him in the lap of luxury for the rest of his life.

Chapter Twenty

Cornish and her team reconvened to go over what they had found.

'No fingerprints other than Elliot Abbotts were found on the weapon. What else have we found?' asked Cornish, irritation in her voice.

Hutchens gave a slight shake of her head.

'We went through the staff rota and found out who was on duty that evening. Callum Roberts had added on several staff members who weren't present. None of the staff working that night noticed anything unusual. All the staff have worked there for years so I can't see it being any of them.'

'Then the assumption is that the killer was one of the guests,' continued Cornish. 'We now know the names of the two missing guests. They weren't together, and Callum Roberts added them on to two different parties to even out the numbers. That was the explanation given to the other guests in the parties, but quite what the reason was for them requesting an invitation in the first place we'll have to find out.'

Cornish wrote the names on the whiteboard.

Charles Rapier and Ashley Roberts.

'What else do we know about Elliot Abbott?' Cornish asked as she took a long gulp of coffee.

Mac brought the team up to speed.

'Elliot Abbott is one-half of Abbott and Abbott estate agents. They've been in business for twenty-five years. They have built up a solid reputation, especially in the higher end of the property market. They command and demand top prices for the properties they market and sell. Elliot's seven years younger than Maxwell Abbott. Maxwell established the estate agency and is in charge. Both are married, Maxwell Abbott married his childhood sweetheart and has five children, whereas Elliot is on his second wife. She has three children, none of which are his. Speaking to the staff in their office, both brothers are quite pushy and particular about the clients they take on. Rumour has it that Elliot Abbott likes to mix business with pleasure and has had several flings. He likes the ladies if you know what I mean.'

'What about the ex-wife? Find out what she knows. Why did she divorce Elliot Abbott? After all, he's worth a pretty penny,' Cornish suspected.

'What do we know about the second wife?'

Hutchens looked up from her notes and spoke.

'Marie Abbott has three children and owns the house they live in. The ex-husband bought it for her. On paper, Elliot Abbott doesn't own any properties. All his money appears to be in the business with his brother. I believe he had to invest a substantial sum in obtaining forty-nine per cent of the shares. His brother owns the controlling share and is very much in charge of the decisions and the day to day running of the limited company. Any other money Elliot Abbott has is invested in a company called Fairmont LLC which has several directors. Interestingly, and until recently, they were made up of the gentlemen in the party of eight and one other, Charles Rapier.'

A crack of thunder rumbled outside, bouncing off the walls. Pearce raised an eyebrow, sending furrows up one half of his forehead. The weather had turned colder with a rainstorm coming in.

DCS Butler had entered the room.

'I know Charles Rapier. I had the pleasure of dealing with him in a previous investigation. Nasty character. Likes to use people. Apparently, he claims he is legit these days. On the surface, it looks that way, but we know he has an underground empire dabbling in drugs. We just can't prove it. He's been too clever to date. But don't underestimate him. Rapier is smart, well-educated and has married well. A fox in sheep's clothing.'

Charles Rapier's name was already on the list and a person of interest.

Cornish had met the likes of Charles Rapier characters before. Smooth like a greased marble sliding across the floor. Difficult to grab hold of. Always above suspicion, and never where the action was, so you couldn't pin anything on them. He made Cornish uneasy. Why would Rapier want to attend the Halloween ball? What did he have to gain? If Rapier had intended to kill Elliot Abbott, then he would have been elsewhere and not in the same room. Yet he skulked away. Cornish meant to find out.

'Pearce, you and I will pay Charles Rapier a visit. I want to know exactly what he was doing at Holland House. Hutchens and I will then visit Ashley Roberts._Mac, check out all those recently released from prison and in Cornwall._There can't be too many down here.

It was then that the rumble of thunder exploded. Except it wasn't thunder. They all looked out the window of the operation room in Pydar House, Truro, and saw flames and smoke in the sky.

Chapter Twenty-One

The explosion could be heard from a distance. People assumed it had been a gas leak.

Penpol wasn't used to such attention from the police and the press. A picturesque Creekside village in the parish of Feock, not far from Carrick Roads, Penpol, was an exclusive area occupied by those with deeper pockets. Popular with the boating fraternity and near to Loe Beach where there was a sailing school. The beautiful Restronguet Creek opened up onto the Carrick Roads, Fal Estuary, and some of the most sheltered sailing waters anywhere in the United Kingdom. And, only a five-minute drive to Cornwall's capital city, Truro.

Cornish stepped out of her VW and took in her first impression of the elevated countryside views from Penpol. The day had started overcast in Truro, but here only a few miles down the road, it was bright and sunny with a slight chill in the air. Now a plume of black smoke billowed in the sky. And the car, on fire, appeared to be melting into the tarmac. There were people home, and children were on a half-term week break. The few neighbours, mostly retired, had come out of their big houses, all up and down the normally quiet leafy lane, and were chatting with each other. A couple of people had taken photographs from the driveway, and video footage with their mobile phones and Cornish wanted those images. She suspected there wouldn't be much to see from their angles of vision, but they might have caught a vehicle passing along the road or a stranger in their midst. Her team had ordered the curious people back from the driveway, and DC Mac was in charge of stopping them straying too close.

The Cornwall Fire and Rescue Service was busy extinguishing the flames on the Range Rover, and most of the excitement seemed to be over. Cornish didn't see the need to evacuate anybody from their homes. The properties were spaced well away from each other.

No one had seen anything much or at least remembered any strangers milling around Penpol. The houses were all set back from the main road, with their own drives. The only possibility of anyone spotting anything would be from Tresco House, the sole property in the line of sight.

DC Mac was standing in front of blue and white Police Do Not Cross tape, strung loosely across the entrance immediately onto Judge Mercer's property. DC Mac stood with his hands buried deep inside the pockets of his fluorescent jacket. The Judge wouldn't be going anywhere today.

'Looks like the car caught fire and the gas tank must have exploded,' Pearce explained sensibly.

'Let's wait and see what forensics find out,' said Cornish.

The Forensic Fire and Explosion Investigators were on the scene. The chief investigator from Camborne approached Cornish and confirmed a device had triggered the explosion. They swiftly established it was a car bomb. A nice one. It hadn't been particularly well concealed.

DCI Cornish had only ever dealt with one other bomb exploding before. It wasn't a common occurrence in Cornwall.

Confirming his findings to Cornish, the chief investigator explained.

'The bomb would have done the judge and his wife some serious damage if they'd been in the car. As it turned out, the bomb went off prematurely. My guess is, the bomb had a timer set to go off when the Judge should have been in the car. He missed being blown to kingdom come by the fact that he had been delayed leaving the house this morning by fifteen minutes.'

There was no denying the explosion had sounded impressive. Cornish ducked under the tape and walked towards the house with Pearce once the fire was under control and they could pass safely. DCI Cornish shook hands with Judge Mercer as he led them into his office.

'I was wondering when the police would make an appearance.'

'Health and safety, sir. We had to wait for the fire service to control the scene I'm afraid. Are you and Mrs Mercer, alright?' enquired Cornish.

'Do you need a doctor?'

'We're fine. My wife's slightly shaken. Anyway,' he continued, 'now that you're finally here, you'd better come over and take a look.'

Cornish and Pearce followed Judge Mercer over to his desk.

'Of course,' the Judge said, looking first at Cornish, then Pearce, 'I was going to call Chief Constable Jane Falconbridge this morning after my court case. I received this threat on Saturday morning, and I'm assuming that what is left of my car is the result.'

Half listening, Cornish read the note. This was no warning. The Judge had clearly upset someone. Cornish wanted to check Judge Mercer's cases old and new. Had anybody been released from prison recently that the Judge had sentenced? The only thing she knew for sure was that it hadn't been a random act. It was not a reassuring thought.

It had been a gift exclusively meant for the judge or failing him, his wife.

The immediate neighbours shared the driveway of the lane, and Cornish and Hutchens walked up the drive to the main entrance. When the address had come through to Cornish, her curiosity was piqued. This was too much of a coincidence. Jason and Becky Keane owned Tresco House.

Cornish and Hutchens were impressed by the Hollywood Hills style residence. Becky Keane opened the door, and Cornish introduced herself and DS Hutchens. Becky had recognised DCI Cornish straightaway. She led them through to the kitchen via the interconnecting glazed link between the wings of the house. It was a quite astounding open-plan kitchen Cornish had ever seen that curved gently from one end to the other creating visual drama. With its exposed timber and steel structure and vast amounts of glass along two sides, and roof windows in the vaulted ceiling, light streamed in. Taking in the elegant kitchen with Silestone worktops, state-of-the-art equipment, and a big Venetian glass chandelier. This was the type of house Cornish could envisage being on Grand Designs. Electric blinds closed off the glass walls for security and a complete lockdown if necessary. In a house like this, Cornish expected to see a cook or a housekeeper.

Hutchens glanced around the elegant room as Cornish observed Becky Keane. She looked very normal and relaxed for someone who had just heard the explosion.

Becky noticed that both detectives were taking everything in and studying her as well. She may have given the impression of calmness, but inside, Becky was far from relaxed. So far, DCI

Cornish was the only one talking. The other, DS Hutchens, said nothing except gaze around the kitchen.

Cornish was pleasant and polite, trying to put Becky at ease. Cornish was watching Becky, who intrigued her. Cornish sensed Becky Keane had been expecting a visit and not because of the explosion. There was something else.

Cornish spotted a family photograph from the corner of her eye and ground to a halt before turning and picking up the frame to get a better look. They made a lovely family, all smiles.

'Is your husband home?' Cornish asked.

'No,' replied Becky.

'Did you go outside before you heard the explosion? Did your children see or hear anything?'

The questions were coming thick and fast.

'The girls were inside watching TV in the lounge when we heard the explosion,' said Becky.

'Was anyone else in the house with you when you heard the explosion?'

'Only the girls,' replied Becky.

'Would you mind if we asked them a couple of questions?'

'No, that's fine. I'll go and get them.'

As an afterthought, Becky turned and asked if both detectives would like something to drink. Cornish shook her head for both of them and thanked her. She had the bladder of an unruly golf ball.

Becky's two girls had never seen a detective up close and were intrigued.

'Are you going to arrest us?' They looked scared and hopeful. It would be something to tell their classmates.

Cornish and Hutchens smiled. Out of the mouth of innocent children who were sure it was a bomb they had heard, just like on the television. DS Hutchens was good with children and instantly put the two little girls at ease. She asked their names and how old they were.

'My name's Sienna, I'm ten, and my sister Lowenna is seven. Was it a bomb?' Sienna asked, eager to know.

'Maybe,' Cornish said honestly. We aren't sure yet. We have to bring in some special people to check it out. They will look over the car pretty thoroughly. You'd be surprised what they can find out. Cornish smiled; she didn't tell the girls that they already knew it was a bomb. There was no point in frightening them and their parents. Cornish was more interested in finding out who and why someone had planted the bomb in their neighbours.

'I don't suppose either of you went outside earlier,' said Cornish gently to the girls. It seemed unlikely without their mother knowing but Lowenna looked over at Sienna and whispered.

'You aren't in trouble,' said Becky to her daughters. 'The Detective just wants to know if you saw anything or anyone. I won't be angry, I promise.'

'I looked out of the window,' said Sienna tentatively. 'The TV was kind of boring. That's when I saw him. A tall man walking away from Mr and Mrs Mercer. He got into a big truck and drove away.'

'Do you think it was meant for Judge Mercer if it was a bomb?' Becky asked with fresh interest.

'Probably not,' replied Cornish.
Becky didn't believe her. There were too many police cars on the scene, and she knew how important her neighbour was.

Cornish reassured Becky that neither Judge Mercer nor his wife was injured. Still, Cornish knew the attack had scared the judge's wife who was in the house when the incident occurred. The Judge had been out walking their dog before he was due in court later that day. Cornish suspected the bomb was meant for the Judge. He was a well-respected member of the bar. Judge Mercer had featured prominently in some of the highest-profile cases Cornwall's courts had ever seen. As a circuit judge, he was often resident at Exeter Combined Court. Cornish knew him well and considered him an intelligent, determined and fair advocate. Those qualities had stuck with him throughout his successful career because he did his job properly.

Cornish and Hutchens left Becky and the children and walked back down the drive to join Pearce and Mac. But not before Cornish mentioned that she would be back to talk to Becky about the Holland House murder.

Becky watched the Detective walk back to her neighbours. She was worried. Since the murder of Elliot Abbott, ten days earlier, she had a feeling of foreboding and the overwhelming sense of disquiet. Becky had thought in the comfort of her own home, she would be safe, and everything would be all right in the world. Now she wasn't so sure.

Chapter Twenty-Two

Glan Morgan muted the evening news and paced the living room floor. What the hell had just happened. Glan ran an agitated hand through his hair. First, someone had just killed his ex-wife's husband, and now a car bomb had exploded next door to Jason and Becky Keane. It was all over the news, and the judge's place had been heaving with the press earlier. The area around Jason and Becky Keane's neighbours was cordoned off. The Range Rover or what was left of it had been taken away, and a police car was routinely checking the area and Judge Mercer. That would make surveillance harder.

Glan didn't believe in coincidences, and he wondered if Rapier knew and what he was up to. Rapier was a maniac. Glan wondered if he should warn Marie of the danger to his children. Rapier was capable of anything, he knew that. And Glan wanted none of these children hurt, neither his nor the Keane's.

He called Charles Rapier from his burner phone. Rapier denied knowing anything about the car bomb. For the moment Glan believed him. If Rapier didn't arrange the car bomb then who did? Glan couldn't afford for Rapier to think he couldn't be trusted. Rapier wouldn't hesitate to take revenge.

Rapier wanted to know that everything was all set. He didn't want anything else going wrong. They needed to act soon. Glan knew that the Keane's were usually out on Saturday nights. They had a regular babysitter. He hoped this scare wouldn't put them off.

Glan Morgan had casually mentioned to Rapier that Jason and Becky Keane had no cleaner or cook that came in regularly except when they were entertaining.

Everything was on schedule so far. Glan assured Rapier that there were no problems his end. Foy and Fisher were playing their part and Foy had got the guns. Glan hoped they wouldn't be needed.

For everyone's sake.

Chapter Twenty-Three

Cornish thought everyone had left for the day. Then she realised she was not alone. Danielle Butler was lurking in the shadows. They looked at each other for a long moment, and the expression on Cornish's face froze. They were completely alone, and it was getting late.

'Is there something you want to ask me, DCI Cornish?'

In her mind, Claire wanted to ask when Danielle Butler would be leaving Devon and Cornwall Police. The sooner, the better as far as Claire was concerned.

Instead, she said, 'No. I'm not thinking anything. I just want to go home. It's been a long day, a long week. I'm tired.'

Tired of you, thought Cornish.

'Why don't you stay awhile and tell me how Operation Holland is coming along?'

Cornish heard the words, but her eyes held a different message as she observed DCS Butler watch her like a predator. They stood facing one another before Cornish turned and walked out of the building with purpose. She had no intention of starting any discussion.

Danielle Butler watched Cornish exit with grim determination. Her plan was getting closer. Soon Jamie Nance would be hers.

Danielle Butler stepped into her townhouse. She'd always fancied this part of the country. She could see herself settling down with the right man and even having children. Danielle Butler was ambitious and independent, but she wanted more from her life. She wanted what Claire Cornish had, and it was time to strike. Danielle Butler smiled at her reflection in the mirror. She had never considered marrying before, but now that Claire Cornish had a fiancée that was all that mattered.

Desire was a powerful motivating force, and what she wanted was getting nearer, closing the gap between her and her quarry.

The smile died on Claire's lips as she thought about her confrontation with DCS Danielle Butler as she drove home. Claire hadn't wanted the position herself, and now she was stuck with Butler as her immediate boss, one she didn't like and didn't trust. Cornish had spent twenty-five years carving out her career and considered herself to be a damn good murder detective. The last thing she wanted was for it to be destroyed by Butler.

Jamie had told her she had nothing to worry about.

'Anybody ever told you, you're the suspicious sort?'

Claire hoped that was true.

Jamie wrapped his arms around Claire as she sank onto the sofa next to him. Englebert wasn't impressed at having to give up his spot. Until recently, he had been the only beating heart that Claire truly adored, but he now had to share the limelight. Jamie kissed the top of Claire's head as they all snuggled up together. They were now a team of three in Honeysuckle cottage.

They watched the television for a while each in their own thoughts. The bombing in Penpol had been headline news for the week and Claire was pleased to see Jamie rock up on Friday evening. It now felt quite empty when he wasn't there. Even Englebert appeared to be sad when Jamie left after the weekend. Claire didn't know what she would do without Jamie in her life. Jamie insisted she would be just fine, but that was before he had come back into her life. Claire was a strong person but falling in love had made her feel weak and defenceless at times. Claire hadn't realised just how vulnerable she had become in such a short time. Emotions could do that to you. She knew Jamie would never hurt her, but she was suddenly very aware of how fragile life could be, and she didn't want what they had, which was now so precious, to be destroyed. Jamie didn't understand why Claire felt this way, but then he didn't have a clue about Danielle Butler. If he had been aware of her existence, then he would have understood Claire's obvious concerns.

Reassuring her, Jamie leaned over and planted a kiss on her lips.

He silenced her with his lips against hers. Then he heaved her off

the sofa and together they made their way upstairs. Jamie Nance

was the happiest man alive.

Chapter Twenty-Four

Rapier was the first to encounter an unexpected problem. He had paid Callum Roberts well and didn't expect to receive a visit from the police. Callum Roberts had got greedy, and now Rapier's name was in the frame if he didn't cough up the money. Callum Roberts was becoming an inconvenience.

Rapier was sitting in his office in his Cornish home when his wife interrupted him, saying the police wanted a word. He had no idea what they wanted.

DCI Cornish and DS Pearce introduced themselves.

'I believe you paid Callum Roberts to get you on the guestlist for the Halloween Masked Ball, at Holland House in Truro,' Cornish said.

'That's not a crime is it?' replied Rapier facing DCI Cornish while DS Pearce glanced around the sizeable sumptuous office.

'I take it you know Elliot Abbott. He owns the estate agency, Abbott & Abbott, in Truro with his brother. Elliot Abbott was murdered at the Halloween Ball, with a note in his pocket. Still, then you knew that already,' continued Cornish. She was prepared to take a gamble that Rapier had placed the note there. Charles Rapier raised an eyebrow. 'I know of him, why?'

'Well, as I said sir, I think you know him rather well. In fact, until fairly recently you were in business together.'

Straightening up, Rapier removed his glasses and gazed outside surveying the extensive lawns. It had taken him years to build up his fortune, and he wasn't going to be easily separated from it. 'We parted company if that's what you want me to say. Elliot Abbott owes me a lot of money. Why would I want him dead? *At least not yet.*'

Taking a look from Cornish as encouragement Rapier continued.

'If you must know I went there out of idle curiosity. Elliot Abbott was, as usual, lording himself up. He thinks he is important. What the hell has this got to do with anything anyway?' Rapier demanded.

'We wouldn't be doing our job if we didn't ask. Would you mind confirming you placed the note in his pocket, sir.'

Rapier cleared his throat.
'Yes, it was me. I admit that. But I didn't kill him.'

With Cornish's eyes still firmly fixed on his, she added. 'No sir, I believe you didn't. Unless forensics finds evidence to the contrary, then I'd agree.'

As Cornish and Pearce left, Rapier closed his office door and made a call.

Outside Pearce was the first to speak.

'Why go to all that trouble to place a note in Elliot Abbott's pocket?'

'So, Elliot Abbott knew he could get to him anywhere. There is another possibility,' Cornish said. 'He had help.'

'You mean Ashley Roberts?' Said Pearce.

'Possibly.'

As Cornish digested this thought, she dismissed the notion almost immediately.

'There's no evidence to suggest that or proof at the moment. I do, however, think the motive is personal. Rather like a stab in the back. This could be for personal or business reasons. I want you and Mac to look more closely at the business dealings, especially concerning Charles Rapier and Elliot Abbott. I want to have a chat with Ashley Roberts.'

Cornish wanted to know exactly what Ashley Roberts was doing there.

Chapter Twenty-Five

The wooden chalet, Skylark, gave Ashley Roberts a sense of peace for the first time in a long time. Maybe she would be able to handle what life had thrown at her and survive it. She cautiously smiled as she opened the French doors and stepped into the chalet. She needed time to heal, and she had plenty of that.

Ashley Roberts had moved. There was no forwarding address. The only thing Cornish and Hutchens had was an email address and a mobile number from the new owners of Treganatha. But Ashley Roberts wasn't hiding. Cornish dialled the number, and she answered.

Within an hour, Cornish and Hutchens were pulling into the chalet park at Gwithian Towans just outside Gwithian. Ashley Roberts was staying in chalet number seventeen, Skylark. As she slid back the patio doors to greet her visitors, the two police officers introduced themselves.

The rest of the chalet park was empty. With nobody around, the chalet park was closed to the public during the winter season. There was a stack of bills on the table. Ashley had been sorting through them, paying them off with what was left from the proceeds of her home. Ashley Roberts wasn't living an extravagant lifestyle. She wasn't even complaining about her current state of affairs. Ashley Roberts had resigned herself to her fate. Her ex-husband had had the last laugh, and she hoped he would rot in hell. In reality, Ashley hadn't yet grasped the stark reality and implications of what was happening to her. She felt constantly stressed and uncertain about what the future held. She could only manage the day to day tasks to get through from one day to the next. She couldn't see beyond that.

Ashley couldn't really say why she went to the masked Halloween Ball to DCI Cornish and DS Hutchens. It was an expense she could ill afford, but she wanted to talk to Elliot Abbott and tell him what she intended to do. And she wanted it to be in a public place. The Halloween Ball seemed the obvious choice and opportunity.

Ashley Roberts felt totally isolated. Her children were concerned and worried and had offered her help, but she wouldn't take it. She constantly cried at any given moment over the grief of losing her home and not knowing what will become of her. She felt empty inside, older, worn out by the circumstances. Everything required so much more effort.

Cornish and Hutchens let Ashley Roberts speak and pour her heart out for the next two hours. It had been a long time coming.

Chapter Twenty-Six

Cornish and Hutchens left Ashley Roberts in tears. If Cornish had been the sort of person to find a celestial meaning in the ordinary world, she might have said it would be nature, in all its glory, that would heal Ashley Roberts broken soul. The habitat of golden soft sand dunes and grassland of the Towans offered some protection to the chalets from the fierce Atlantic storms.

Ashley Roberts was not capable of murder. She wasn't sure that DCI Cornish Believed her. She might have wanted Elliot Abbott dead and may have thought herself capable, but the reality was very different. She was pleased he had been killed, but she hadn't been the one to take his life. Ashley Roberts was angry with the world, and her own stupidity and foolishness. She had paid a heavy price for that already and was a broken woman. Ashley made no attempt to move when Cornish and Hutchens got up to leave. Only then did she offer the briefest of acknowledgement that their visit was over. After the detailed discussion, Cornish was satisfied that Ashley Roberts was innocent, and the police needed to focus their attention elsewhere.

Marie Abbott was surprised by a visit from the police. She had been busy preparing the funeral arrangements for her husband when Cornish and Hutchens showed up. Elliot Abbott's body had been released, and the funeral was due to take place at the end of the week. On the pretence of informing Marie Abbott that she would be attending the funeral on behalf of the police, Cornish wanted an informal chat with the widow. And to pass on their condolences.

Marie Abbott showed the two policewomen into the lounge and offered them tea. Cornish declined, once again, for both of them. Glancing around the room, there were plenty of photographs of the couple in happier times.

'All I have are memories now,' Marie sighed. She looked over at Cornish and Hutchens and thought about her life in Cornwall and

London, a lifetime ago. The media had been camped at her door since her husband's death. Hoping to get a story and a picture of her and the children.

'Do you have any idea who would want to kill your husband?' asked Cornish injecting the right note of sympathy in her voice.

Marie Abbott shook her head sadly.

Chapter Twenty-Seven

Annette Abbott hesitated when she saw DCI Cornish and DS Hutchens standing on her doorstep. She wanted to tell the police to bugger off and leave her alone. The press had scattered like rats when she had told them to piss off earlier in the week. The last thing she wanted to be reminded of was her ex-husband. She didn't really want to go to his funeral. Other than to see him enter the gates of hell.

Annette Abbott had been at the Halloween Ball with another party. She admitted their paths still crossed occasionally but where possible she tried to avoid any contact with her ex-husband.

Cornish and Hutchens looked at each other, noting the frisson of hatred that was palpable even to an outsider. Cornish wanted to know why.

'What's the story, then between you and your ex-husband?'

Annette Abbott considered the question for a few minutes before answering.

'Elliot Abbott is a rat,' Annette Abbott said succinctly. Of the highest order, if you must know. I found out his dirty little secret.'

It wasn't hard for Cornish and Hutchens to draw a conclusion from that. Each fell silent, preparing themselves for what was to come. Sure enough, Annette Abbott spilt the beans on her husband's activities. The evidence was still sitting on her desktop computer.

Cornish and Hutchens's faces betrayed very little of the emotions swirling through their bodies as they listened to what Annette Abbott had to say. Rage flooded through Annette Abbott's veins as she imagined what Elliot Abbott had done throughout his life and the lives wasted and abused by him. Cornish and Hutchens nodded sombrely; it was evident that Annette Abbott's emotional wounds would never heal. Which was why she had felt compelled to visit Marie Abbott and warn her of the danger she was placing her children in.

Cornish cleared her throat. Marie Abbott had failed to mention the visit. She now had a motive for wanting her husband dead if he had been abusing her children. She had given the impression of a good family man and that the marriage was a happy one. Annette Abbott's version of events and circumstances leaned towards a different story.

Chapter Twenty-Eight

Becky Keane had dreaded this second visit. Cornish and Hutchens were doing the rounds, and Becky Keane was a loose end Cornish wanted to tie up. Sitting in the kitchen, Becky Keane knew what was coming. Cornish wasn't stupid, and like any other woman, the photographs displayed in the breakfast room told a very different story to real life. Cornish was too astute for Becky to be able to pull the wool over her eyes.

Cornish came straight to the point.

'Did you have an affair with Elliot Abbott?'

'Yes. I discovered my husband had been having an affair, and I wanted to get my own back. Except my husband failed to even notice. When I realised what Elliot Abbott was like I called the whole thing off. He was here under my roof, as he had been on many occasions, with my children here. I put their lives at risk. I feel responsible. And stupid. Yes, I wanted Elliot Abbott out of my life and that of my family's. But I didn't kill him.' Tears spilt over. If my husband knew he would be devastated. Please don't tell him,' pleaded Becky Keane.

Cornish decided to hold her tongue rather than raise the prospect that potentially Jason Keane was very aware of the affair and had confronted Elliot Abbott about it. Had he known just what Elliot Abbott was capable of then he had a motive for wanting him dead.

Cornish told Becky Keane she would need to talk to her husband anyway. He was at the Halloween Ball.

'Is that really necessary, Detective Chief Inspector Cornish?'

'Of course. I understand how you feel, but your husband may know more than you think. We need to speak to him to eliminate him from our enquiries. I'm afraid this may all come out. You say your husband had an affair? Who was that with?'

Becky Keane handed Cornish the photographs of her husband with one of her closest friends.

'My husband has no idea, I know. If this gets out, it will be splashed over all the papers. I'm not bothered about myself, but my husband's been going through a rough time lately, financially, if you know what I mean.'

Cornish and Hutchens looked at the photograph. This case was getting more complicated by the minute.

'Ask your husband to come and see me. Maybe it would be better if we saw him in one of the interview rooms in Truro.'

They weren't eliminating suspects, instead, accumulating them. Ashley Roberts, Annette Abbott, Marie Abbott and Becky Keane all had one thing in common.

They all had a motive for wanting Elliot Abbott dead.

Chapter Twenty-Nine

Pearce and Mac were on their way to meet the alias, Mr Smith, and his partner of twenty-five years, Miss Weston, when he received the call from DCI Cornish. She wanted all those present at the Halloween Ball in the Abbott & Abbott party to be interviewed before the funeral. Given this new development, Pearce now had a photograph on his phone that was going to stir up a hornet's nest in the Smith and Weston household. He smiled amused at the alias the couple had given themselves.

They drove up the single track road to the large fifteenth-century farmhouse just outside Wadebridge. It wasn't what either of them had expected. Surrounded by its own gardens and fields, the granite farmhouse didn't exude the wealth of its occupants. This was a completely different life to their previous one of being in the pop charts and mobbed by fans.

Pearce knocked on the main door and heard the squelching of wet footwear approach. Mr Smith's smile dimmed as he recognised Pearce from Holland House and that awful evening.

The two officers sat in the large kitchen at the supersized oak table while Mr Smith changed. He had been surfing earlier. With the formalities out of the way Pearce looked towards Miss Weston and presented the photograph.

'What's this got to do with Elliot Abbott's murder? I don't see a connection,' she replied.

'Well, it came to light during this investigation. Did Elliot Abbott know about your affair?' enquired Pearce.

'Not that I know of,' replied Miss Weston.

Mr Smith lingered in the kitchen doorway for a moment and then stepped inside, curious at the overheard conversation.

'May I,' As he picked up the phone and looked at the cosy couple in the photo.

To the surprise of Pearce and Mac, the retired pop idol smiled.

'This is old news, DS Pearce. Jason and I settled this matter some time ago. You are barking up the wrong tree with this. This happened when Miss Weston and I split up for a few months but now we are very much back together. That was in the past. How did you get this photograph?'

Pearce wondered whether he should give a short answer or a long one. Instead, he asked a question to both of them.

'Does Becky Keane know about this?'

'I can't see how,' replied Miss Weston. We were discreet and met away from our homes. Only the three of us know. Becky's one of my closest friends, and I feel terrible about what happened. I would hate for Becky to find out. It would destroy her. And our friendship.'

It was too late for that, thought Pearce as he continued the questions as Mac glanced around. Smith and Weston didn't live the life of wealth or display it in a garish way. Pearce and Mac came to the same conclusion. They were the least likely to be responsible for Elliot Abbott's death. The couple had no reason to kill him. The business venture they were all involved in had affected them all. And they were unaware of the financial state of Jason and Becky Keane. They assumed Jason and Becky were minted like themselves.

Pearce and Mac relayed their findings to Cornish on their way to see Maxwell Abbott and his wife. It was a dead end.

Cornish mulled over what they had learnt before she spoke.

Looks like we'll have to use our little grey cells.'

Chapter Thirty

Maxwell Abbott was in his office when Pearce and Mac walked in. He was sorting out all the legal paperwork that went with a partner and brother's death in the company. He explained to Pearce and Mac that he was now the sole owner of Abbott &Abbott Estate agency. That had always been the agreement. 'The money paid in by my brother will remain in the business and give Marie a return on her investment for now, but she doesn't have any control in the running of the business. I offered to buy back the shares, but Marie said she was more than happy to receive a decent income.'

Maxwell Abbott gave his statement which hadn't changed since the evening of Elliot's death. He might have been in business with his brother, and they socialised in the same circles occasionally for a good cause. Still, outside of that, he knew very little about his brother, and for that fact, Marie. His wife only mixed when they had a social gathering to go to, but unlike the rest of the group they didn't go to each other's homes, and they didn't entertain much at home. He preferred to keep his personal life private.

Pearce and Mac thanked Maxwell Abbott and left. When they arrived at Maxwell's home, his wife was expecting them. Anne Abbott was quiet and homely. She didn't fit in with the likes of Becky Keane and the Miss Weston. She wasn't interested in fame and fortune or gracing the front pages of a magazine. Her children and husband were her life.

Anne Abbott watched DS Pearce and DC Mac drive away and wondered what it would be like to have somebody look at her like her husband looked at Becky Keane and her stupid bitch best friend.

Chapter Thirty-One

Jason Keane sat opposite Cornish and Pearce in the interview room. He wasn't under caution.

'As far as I can see, there are eight potential suspects, and you are one of them, Mr Keane. You have a motive.'

'Fair point, but I didn't kill Elliot Abbott. Why would I?' Jason Keane said, as he sat back in the chair ruffling his hair.

'You tell us, Mr Keane. You knew about your wife's affair, didn't you?'

'Now hang on a minute. I didn't do anything to Elliot if that's what you are trying to imply.'

Cornish tried a different tact. She wanted to get an angle on their working relationship, and Jason Keane reiterated what his wife had said earlier when questioned. Jason didn't want the world to know of their financial situation. They would weather the storm, and he would soon be back on top. Cornish mentioned Rapier and Jason squirmed. Charles Rapier wanted the money owed to him. He had accused them, Jason Keane, Elliot Abbott, Maxwell Abbott and Mr Smith of stealing his share. Nothing could be further from the truth. Jason and the others didn't like Charles Rapier. He would drag them down with his dubious business deals, and they weren't about to trash their reputations.

Cornish shook her head. Jason Keane hadn't let on if he knew what Elliot Abbott was really like and Cornish didn't think for now it was relevant to mention. Like everyone present at the Ball, Jason had heard Marie's screams as the lights came on and Elliot Abbott was lying on the floor. He had been right next to the man, his friend and business partner, and not seen or heard a thing, and it haunted his dreams nightly.

Jason Keane walked out of Pydar House a worried man. He had risked everything, his business and his marriage and for what?

Money. Charles Rapier had made it clear that he wanted his money owed. Still, Jason couldn't believe Rapier would resort to murder. Jason shouldn't have had the affair. That had affected everything. Elliot Abbott had taken advantage of the situation and filled his slippers for a short time. He had wanted to kill him. They were all as bad as each other, which is why nobody had done a thing about it. Everything had returned to normal. Or so he had thought. Now he wasn't so sure.

Chapter Thirty-Two

Elliot Abbott's funeral procession left his home in The Avenue, Truro. It made its way to Penmount Crematorium just outside of the city. Marie Abbott and her three children were in one car. Maxwell Abbott and his wife in the other. The vehicles arrived at Trelawny Chapel, one of the two chapels on the grounds. Trelawny Chapel was the biggest with seating for just over a hundred people. Not as intimate as Kernow Chapel but the turnout was expected to be high.

On arrival, the coffin was transferred from the hearse to the panelled-oak wheeled bier. This preceded the mourners into the Chapel and was placed within the catafalque. Marie Abbott followed the coffin, her gaze transfixed ahead. The service was filled with people who had been in business with Elliot Abbott. If they had known about his secret life, the church would have been empty.

At the moment of committal, the curtains were drawn, the coffin hidden from view until the mourners left the chapel. Elliot's remains were to be placed in one of the family plots.

Cornish observed Marie Abbott putting on a brave face. It brought back memories of all the countless and sometimes pointless funerals she had attended throughout her career and personal life. Where were these so-called perfect families that existed? No one escaped the real clutches of life. Even the church admitted the perfect family didn't exist, and there were no perfect husbands or ideal wives or in-laws. Everyone had secrets, some secrets were worse than others. Human beings were flawed, and for that reason alone, Cornish knew she would catch the murderer.

Jason Keane was a broken man financially. Becky had hidden her affair from him during their marriage, but Jason knew. The day of the Halloween Ball and Elliot's death they'd had an awful row, and they'd both said things in anger which they now regretted.

Becky hadn't wanted to go to the Ball because of Elliot Abbott.

When Jason found out exactly what Elliot was like, he had

wanted to kill him.

Becky sat solemnly beside her husband. Elliot had been murdered

by one of them as far as she was concerned. She was certain DCI

Cornish was there to determine who that was.

Maxwell Abbott and Anne Abbott sat silently each with their

own thoughts. He took her hand and gave it a quick, reassuring

squeeze.

'He's gone now.'

Maxwell and his brother had never truly seen eye to eye. Still,

family was important, and as the saying goes, blood is thicker

than water. Whatever Maxwell's misgivings about his brother, he

was still his kin. The rumour mill was just that. Elliot had many

masks, and you could ask a dozen people the same question and

get twelve different opinions about him.

Anne Abbott felt relief that her brother-in-law had died. She had never trusted him around her children. There was something about Elliot that had made her skin crawl. Having a genuine distrust for most people, she now looked at her husband and asked herself the question. Was Maxwell Abbott capable of murder?

Annette silently wept as her ex-husband's coffin made its final journey. She had been devastated and hurt during her marriage to Elliot. There was a darkness to him that she had sensed every single day she had been married. There was indeed a God. Elliot had finally paid the price.

Charles Rapier felt nothing for Elliot Abbott. He never had and never would. In fact, he disliked all of them, here today, grieving for a business colleague and a close friend. One of them was a murderer. He wanted them all dead and in hell. He wanted his money.

Ashley Roberts sat at the back of the chapel. She wanted to see Elliot Abbott enter the furnace. Ashley had expected to feel some sort of relief at his passing, but she didn't. Instead, she felt cheated. Elliot Abbott had got away with his crimes, and Ashley Roberts realised she would never get the closure she wanted. Ashley had lived with the pain and hurt. Until the day had arrived when there was an opportunity to balance the scales. Ashley had missed her chance and knew she wasn't the only one present in the chapel that had wanted Elliot Abbott dead. That in itself was a comforting thought. They were all too entrenched in their past mistakes.

Glan Morgan sat in the shadows amongst the rest of the mourners. He was there for Marie and his children. He saw Charles Rapier up at the front in all his pompous glory. Glan watched Jason and Becky Keane, Maxwell Abbott and his mousy wife and the popstar couple. All huddled together surreptitiously, he wondered, which one of them had killed Elliot Abbott.

Callum Roberts attended Elliot Abbott's funeral since the poor man had died on his watch at Holland House. More importantly, he wanted to make an appearance to remind the killer that he was still waiting for his money.

Cornish observed Elliot Abbott's family and the rest of the mourners. There was no better way to smoke out a killer.
As Cornish watched the family, she realised that they were all guilty of something. They all had hidden secrets.

Cornish observed the mourners file out from the church and wondered who the man was that had caught Marie Abbott's eye as he walked away from the crowd. Cornish had noticed Marie Abbott acknowledge Glan Morgan's presence as he silently retreated back to his car and drove away. No one else had seen Glan Morgan except Charles Rapier. He made a mental note to himself to warn Glan Morgan again of what would happen to his family if the plan failed.

The reception was held in Mannings in Truro so that colleagues could pop in and pay their respects. Marie had arranged the catering. It was the least she could do. There was a full spread of delicious canapes and pastries. The mourners wouldn't forget Elliot Abbott's funeral in a hurry.

Cornish walked the room listening to threads of conversations hoping to catch something said, a slip of the tongue. She made her way over to Marie Abbott and extended the condolences of the police force. When Marie Abbott spoke, her voice was entirely devoid of emotion, her eyes completely shuttered. Cornish assumed she was still in shock. Marie Abbott was now a wealthy widow, and as Cornish left the wake, Marie Abbott watched her go. Then again, if you decide to make a deal with the devil, a little awkwardness was to be expected.

Had Glan Morgan been at the wake or Cornish stayed five minutes longer, she would have observed with her sharp eye the recognition between two of the mourners.

Chapter Thirty-Three

It had been one hell of a week for Cornish and her team and by the end of Friday Cornish was looking forward to having a few hours to herself. Jamie had taken the afternoon off and driven down to Cornwall. He wanted to surprise Claire.

DCS Butler watched Cornish's face soften as Jamie flipped into the office. As Claire waved him off, Danielle Butler wondered what it would be like to have somebody look at her with even a tenth of that affection.

The case was proving to be more interesting by the day. The team were fully assembled in the operation room, and Cornish wanted to know what everybody had found out.

Cornish pointed to the faces on the wall. One of them was their killer, she was sure of that. But who was it? They all had a motive and were all present. Cornish watched her team look from one face to the other.

'We've covered everyone's movements on the night of the Halloween Ball, and spoken to them since. What have we learnt? Anybody is capable of killing, given the right motivation. Callum Roberts fiddles the books, we know that. And he's hiding something. I don't believe the cameras weren't on that night. Callum Roberts is an opportunist and likes fancy things. I wouldn't put it past him to blackmail the killer. Also, there were two extra guests at the Ball, Charles Rapier and Ashley Roberts. Neither killed Elliot Abbott. Charles Rapier would be pretty stupid to get an invitation and take his revenge in public. Like he said, he would have made sure he had an alibi. Ashley Roberts doesn't appear to have what it takes to take a man's life, although she does have a strong motive.'

DS Hutchens spoke.

'What about the knife. It belonged to Elliot Abbott and the only people who knew that was Annette Abbott and Marie Abbott. Knife crime can often be a personal crime.'

'My thoughts exactly,' Cornish couldn't resist adding. 'If we take that thought process a little further, the only person to gain from Elliot Abbott's death is Marie Abbott.'

Cornish paused before continuing.

'The problem is we have no proof, no evidence. Elliot Abbott is according to even his closest friends and colleagues and after delving into his history with a fine-toothed comb, a distasteful, smart bugger. Who probably deserved what he got. Still, in the eyes of the law, a crime has been committed. Someone must pay.'

Pearce spoke up.

'Do you think Elliot Abbott's death and the bomb are connected?'

'I'm trying to figure out the connection, join the dots together. We are missing something, and I wish I knew what it was,' replied Cornish.

Mac held his hands up. All conversation stopped as the team turned to him.

'Well, um, I have the list of those released recently from prison and in our area. Glan Morgan and James Foy were both released on the same day from HMP Exeter Ma'am. I thought you'd like to know. Glan Morgan is Marie Abbott's ex-husband. And he used to work for Charles Rapier.'

They had just stumbled on a huge clue.

Pearce gave Mac a clap on the back and Cornish wrote Glan Morgan's name on the wall.

'Maybe Glan Morgan found out from Marie what kind of man Elliot Abbott was and decided to take him out of the picture,' laughed Pearce.

'Well, I'm just saying, it's possible.'

Cornish addressed Mac.

'Find out where Glan Morgan is living and let's check out his alibi.'

'I'm already on it. He's not where he's supposed to be. He disappeared just before the Halloween Ball.'

Glan Morgan was suddenly someone of particular importance to the case. 'No one knows where he is,' Mac answered. 'He's completely disappeared.'

'Well, that's what we need to find out,' replied Cornish.

Chapter Thirty-Four

Claire walked into Honeysuckle Cottage. The fire burning was a welcome sight as was Jamie leafing through a hefty-looking textbook.

'Hi,' Claire murmured, leaning over Jamie.

'Hi, yourself,' he leaned back and stretched out his arm, pulling Claire over and planting a kiss on her upturned face. Claire chuckled.

'Do you know what I love about you, DCI Cornish?'

Jamie smiled as Claire replied.

'My intelligence?'

'Apart from that.' Jamie wrapped his arms around Claire and drew her into the warmth of his body.

'You gave us a second chance.'

Claire smiled.

'We gave each other a chance, and Bonnie.'

Claire sat down next to Jamie on the sofa. They had arranged to speak to Bonnie over the weekend, and Bonnie had promised to visit. They were all afraid, just in case, things didn't work out. It was an admission that gave her cause for concern. There weren't all happy endings, like in the movies. This was real life, and anything could happen.

Jamie looked at Claire and saw the makings of fear already beginning to mar the happiness they'd found. His hand tightened on hers, and he raised Claire's hand to his lips to press a kiss against her palm. That's what he loved about Claire, her empathy and kindness towards others. Jamie would never let anybody hurt her.

As Claire looked at Jamie, she thought privately that it was not herself she was worried about. Who was there to watch over Jamie and Bonnie?

Claire had a terrible premonition that their happiness would be short-lived, and she tried to banish this from her thoughts when she woke up the following morning.

Together they walked the headland with Englebert. The pace was slow as Englebert sniffed everything. Sure enough, the Autumn weather was like a blast of cold air as the wind chill factor increased its effectiveness. Holding hands, Claire and Jamie felt like a young courting couple. Staring out to sea each with their own thoughts, Claire realised how much she loved her life and Cornwall. Jamie now saw Cornwall through her eyes, and he felt the same. He was home.

Work was never far from Claire's thoughts. While Callum Roberts had been paid a generous salary by his employer, it was nowhere near enough to fund the kind of lifestyle he enjoyed. He had managed to generate the extra income from his scams. Had there not been a murder that night, Callum Roberts would have continued his ways undiscovered, for possibly many years and maybe forever. Likewise, all the hidden secrets which were slowly seeping to the surface might have remained buried. Cornish blew out a long breath. They had possibly stumbled onto something far bigger and complex. But, just, how big?

Chapter Thirty-Five

When James Foy heard on the news that Judge Mercer's car had been blown up, he knew he would be a suspect. It didn't take the police long to track him down to his bedsit in Holmbush.

Foy opened the door to DCI Cornish.

'What brings you here?' Foy asked, although he already knew.

'A little incident in Penpol. Someone tried to blow up Judge Mercer. You may remember the name,' she said, looking Foy in the eye.

'Yes, I do. Couldn't happen to a nicer person,' Foy said without hesitating.

'Wish I'd had the balls to do it myself. But he's not worth going back to prison for. Is he dead?' he asked hopefully.

'Fortunately, not. But whoever did it narrowly missed.'

'That's a shame,' Foy replied, unconcerned.

'Where were you yesterday, by the way?' Cornish asked.

'Here, and in St Austell. Seeing my parole officer,' Foy replied.

Cornish observed Foy, who looked totally unconcerned as he gave them his parole officer's details. Cornish and Pearce drove away as Foy watched the police officers leave. That had been a lucky escape.

Foy turned back to go over the plan once more.

Cornish didn't like James Foy. He was all bad, but he wasn't stupid. Foy was more than capable of setting a bomb.

'Maybe the Keane girl will recognise his photograph on file. You never know,' said Pearce.

'It can't hurt,' Cornish agreed, nodding and thinking about James Foy.

James Foy had spent most of his life inside one institution or another, and he was far more dangerous now he was out. Released early for good behaviour and saving a prison officers life, Cornish was not convinced he would keep his nose clean. Men like him rarely stayed free for long.

Cornish and Pearce drove in silence for a while thinking about the possible list of suspects capable of placing a car bomb under Judge Mercer's car. In Cornwall, the list wasn't too long, and they knew for sure someone had meant to kill the judge.

Chapter Thirty-Six

Charles Rapier would be out of the country before the kidnapping. Rapier had no intention of being a suspect, he was smarter than that. He knew that Glan Morgan would expose him given the first opportunity. As long as Morgan did as instructed then his children were safe. Rapier had reminded him of that fact following Elliot Abbott's funeral.

Glan Morgan had no clue about Rapier's other plan which had now backfired with Elliot Abbott's death. That was somewhat inconvenient. Rapier still held all the cards. Glan Morgan had no idea that he was a pawn in Rapier's game. Elliot Abbott was dead, and Keane would now have to pay up, without question. Rapier was the boss of all he controlled. He placed the files back in his safe. Glan Morgan's file was among them, and a further two had been added, James Foy and Miles Fisher. If Rapier was caught, then they would all join him in prison.

Charles Rapier was already leveraged heavily financially with his business. No bank was prepared to lend him the funds he needed. He wanted his money. The last thing Rapier had needed was some prick setting off a bomb at Judge Mercer's home. Rapier didn't believe in coincidences, especially when they happened on the same street. Over the years, Rapier had learnt to trust his gut instinct. It had served him well and hadn't let him down before. That was why he had chosen Morgan in the first place. He wasn't the usual type of villain you found behind bars. Rapier was beginning to think one of Glan Morgan's accomplices had figured on killing two birds with one stone. That was the most likely situation, and if he could figure that out, then the police wouldn't be far behind after the kidnapping. Rapier had to be one step ahead of them all the time.

Chapter Thirty-Seven

Cornish parked her VW in the driveway and her and Pearce walked up to the front door. The disturbing evidence found in Glan Morgan's flat had been enough to convince Cornish that Jason and Becky Keane and their children were in possible danger.

Becky Keane opened the door. Cornish wondered if Morgan and any accomplices were watching the house. Despite that possibility, Cornish made the decision to enter through the front door visibly. Maybe a police presence would make Morgan think again, although, Glan Morgan wasn't aware that the police were looking for him.

Glan Morgan saw the police officers arrive at the Keane residence. He assumed they were there following the death of Elliot Abbott. He had no reason to think otherwise. He was getting slightly paranoid with Rapier on his back all the time. And, he knew the day was coming close to snatching the children. Rapier had left for Europe, on schedule, and their plans hadn't changed. They were as prepared as they would ever be.

Glan Morgan hadn't called Rapier and didn't see the need to bother him now with the police turning up. Rapier had made it clear that Glan was not to contact him, unless he had a problem, even though he was using a burner mobile.

Jason and Becky Keane had no idea why the police had come to see them. They had just finished supper when Cornish and Pearce turned up. Cornish had chosen this time so as not to look suspicious. She had wanted the whole family at home and calling Jason Keane back home during the day would have looked odd if they were being watched.

As Cornish and Hutchens sat down in the kitchen with Jason and Becky, what she was going to say would change their life forever.

'Mr and Mrs Keane, we are working on a hunch, a vague possibility that your family is in danger. I could be wrong, but I don't think I am.'

Becky and Jason Keane held hands as they grasped what was being said. Cornish elaborated.

'This isn't about Elliot Abbott's death. Still, during our investigation we found a link relating to Charles Rapier. And we are aware that he believes you and your friends owe him a lot of money. Right now, we only have a few pieces of the puzzle found at a suspect's flat, but we don't like what we are seeing. We believe he intends to harm you.'

Jason looked at Cornish and Pearce and then asked earnestly, 'What does he want?'

'At the moment we don't know, but my guess is, Rapier wants his money.'

'I told him we don't have it. The consortium is currently at rock bottom,' Jason Keane was quick to point out.

Jason Keane found the idea of money amusing as he explained to Cornish and Pearce in the strictest confidence, their financial situation.

'I don't have any money other than what's left in the houses. We have lost everything I made in the last few years. There's nothing left for Rapier to take. I've been selling shares and stocks trying to get back up the ladder, hoping this downturn doesn't last forever. Nobody knows the full depth of our situation, including those close to us. It's not something we want to shout around.'

That was where their life was now, and they were slowly adjusting to it. There were no investments hidden in secret bank accounts. That was why Jason Keane was currently working as a Director for someone else.

'If Rapier thinks he's going to get anything out of me, regardless, he's going to be very disappointed. Maybe someone should tell him,' Jason said as he sat on the sofa.

'Charles Rapier isn't at home. Apparently, he's on holiday, and his secretary doesn't know where,' replied Cornish.
Cornish had no way of getting hold of Rapier. It was a dead end. They couldn't stop what was already in motion. Cornish didn't want to say the actual word, kidnap, to Jason and Becky Keane, but that was what was on her mind. That would send serious alarm bells, and she wanted them to understand that the situation could be potentially dangerous.

'I think Charles Rapier is past asking nicely,' as Cornish told Jason and Becky Keane her thoughts. She searched their faces as she showed them a photograph of Glan Morgan. Neither recognised the name or his face. Cornish asked if the children could look at the picture. It was Sienna who recognised Glan

Morgan. She had seen him walking past the house a few times and in Point.

Cornish didn't want to worry Jason and Becky Keane unduly but now was not the time to downplay what could turn out to be a dangerous situation. Glan Morgan wasn't a violent man on paper, but Rapier was a different matter. He had never been in trouble with the police, but his reputation was well known. Glan Morgan was tied up with Rapier and Cornish could only assume he owed Rapier money. If Glan Morgan was worried for his life and that of his wife and children, then that would be enough to make any man do what Charles Rapier wanted. But the police couldn't find Glan Morgan to ask him.

DC Mac had found out that James Foy had been released from HMP Exeter prison on the same day as Glan. Was Foy connected? If he was, then the situation had just got a lot worse. Cornish showed the family the photograph of Foy and Sienna thought she may have seen him on the day that Judge Mercer's car was blown up.

'Have you noticed anyone watching you, or following you, or acting strangely?'

They shook their heads, but Cornish was sure Glan Morgan and James Foy were working together. Foy was dangerous, violent, and he had been sentenced by Judge Mercer. Something was wrong with this picture, and Cornish felt a storm was coming. She didn't like what she was feeling.

Cornish looked directly at Jason and Becky.
'I think that we need to bring in some protection. If there is even a hint of something happening, then a police presence might deter the situation.'

It took a few minutes for Jason and Becky Keane to absorb their predicament and the implications. Cornish called Chief Constable

Jane Falconbridge. This was bigger than Butler. Cornish had to go to the top, and she was very aware of how pissed off DCS Butler would be. Stepping over, her immediate boss would have its own consequences, but time was of the essence and lives at risk.

Cornish updated Jane Falconbridge who agreed to send two firearm officers to Penpol. They would stay with the family. They would alternate with another shift on rotation, two on, two off.

'Two officers, armed, will arrive in the morning. That should keep you safe,' said Cornish with sympathetic eyes.

Jason Keane asked whether they should keep their regular Saturday evening meals out with friends. Cornish thought it would be best to continue their regular routine. Any changes to that might spook Glan Morgan.

As Cornish and Pearce left the family, she wondered whether she was wrong and was overreacting. Pearce hoped that they were for everyone's sake. But if it was going to get ugly, then the extra armed manpower would be necessary. He didn't think Glan Morgan and his associates would be coming to the party empty-handed.

Cornish started her VW tormented by the thought that Glan Morgan was going to try and kidnap at least one of them. One thing she knew for sure. They wanted money from the Keane's, and if they couldn't pay the ransom, then someone could get seriously hurt. From their training, Cornish and Pearce were both aware that in a kidnap, someone could get killed. The probability was high. Either the police, the kidnappers or both. Hopefully, not the abducted. It was a huge risk and no small undertaking for her team.

It was all part of the job.

Chapter Thirty-Eight

Cornish checked in with Jason and Becky Keane first thing in the morning. The two armed response officers were there and briefed. Both were young constables who had completed the firearms course and were now allowed to carry a weapon, a Glock 17 pistol. Constable Shelley and Constable Wakefield took their positions. They would be replaced by Constable Gatehouse and Constable Newton.

The Keane family were in one hell of a situation if Charles Rapier was after them. He would never believe that there was no money.

Cornish and her team were all anxious. Rapier had left the country, and she was sure this had something to do with what was about to happen. If that was the case, then Cornish suspected they wouldn't have to wait long.

In the office, Cornish and her team were coordinating their findings when she received word that DCS Butler wanted to see her.

Cornish knocked on her boss's door and was summoned in.

Butler was in no mood for small talk.

'The fact is, Cornish, I am your superior, and you undermined my authority by going over my head to Chief Constable Jane Falconbridge. What have you got to say for yourself?'

'I acted in the best interests of the Keane family ma'am. I felt this required a direct answer from the Chief Constable and couldn't wait,' said Cornish pragmatically.

What a joke.

The fact was, thought Cornish, that Butler's only motivation was to act in the best interests of Butler.

Danielle Butler didn't say that she had already complained to her CC, Chief Constable Jane Falconbridge. And she'd been told that whatever grudges she held with Cornish she needed to pull her team together in the interests of the department. Butler had wanted to split the team up, flex her muscles, and Jane Falconbridge made it abundantly clear that whatever Butler's motivations, she would toe the line.

Cornish watched Butler's face and wondered why she felt uneasy. Butler abruptly dismissed her. Cornish replied, 'thank you, ma'am, in a voice devoid of emotion as she cast a fulminating glare back over her shoulder as she closed Butler's door.

Jane Falconbridge had opened up a hornet's nest with DCS Butler in charge. When it came down to criminals, she knew Cornish was the right woman for the job. She had an infallible nose for rooting out trouble.

Butler wouldn't be satisfied that she had been dismissed, and Falconbridge hoped Butler wouldn't undermine everything to bolster her own public persona. CC Falconbridge hoped to God she had been right to appoint Danielle Butler to the position of Chief Superintendent.

Pearce detected the triumphant tone in Cornish's voice.

'Everything alright?'

Cornish looked at her team, and a smile touched the corner of her mouth.

'Butler is fuming I went over her head. She's made a complaint to Chief Constable Jane Falconbridge.'

'Does she know you did it deliberately, or she suspects?'

'Suspicion isn't the same as fact,' Cornish pronounced and smiled.

Cornish may have won this battle, but how long would it be before she felt the ground begin to quake beneath her feet.

Chapter Thirty-Nine

The firearm officers were extremely polite. They based themselves in the kitchen and walked the perimeter of the house regularly and checked all doors and windows. They had been sharing the shifts for the past week, and Cornish was beginning to think they had got it wrong.

Becky Keane had offered to make them food and coffee, but they told her it wasn't necessary. At night the alarm was on when everyone was asleep, and Jason had shown the officers how to work it.

No matter how friendly the police officers were, their very presence in the house seemed ominous and made them all nervous. Cornish called round several times to see how things were going.

'How are you all holding up?' Cornish knew it was an incredible amount of pressure, waiting for something to happen.

'Hopefully, it will be over soon.'

'It's horrible. And scary. It's like being in a movie. I will feel happier when I know you have them behind bars,' Becky said with a rueful smile. She was frantic with worry.

Cornish hated to put anyone at risk, but there was no other way. 'It will do you good to get out tonight,' Cornish said thoughtfully. 'The children will be fine with my officers here.'

Jason Keane walked in, having picked up the babysitter. They had to tell her what was going on and hoped she wouldn't be spooked and put off. She was an elderly lady living in their hamlet. Becky had been astute when picking out babysitters. She wanted someone discreet and grandmotherly for their two daughters, and Hilda was perfect. Becky and Jason kissed the girl's good night and walked out the door at the same time as Cornish. Cornish hoped the evening went smoothly. Jason and Becky Keane had been reluctant to leave the girls.

Glan Morgan was on surveillance which was fortunate for the Keane's. Foy would have suspected the police immediately. Glan didn't.

They would be executing their plan in a few days, and all appeared to be normal at Tresco House. All Glan wanted was his money and to get as far away as possible. He knew he had blown it with Marie and his children. James Foy and Miles Fisher were raring to go, it made no difference to them what happened and who got hurt, as long as they got their money.

They had already been paid the promised one hundred thousand pounds each cash up front, and the balance was to be paid out of the ransom. Neither Foy nor Fisher knew Charles Rapier was behind the kidnap. Rapier had made that clear to Morgan. Glan Morgan drove back to his cottage. He knew the exact time they would make their move. They were in no hurry. The plan was set, and there was no reason to think the Keane's would alter their usual routine.

Glan Morgan hadn't been back to his flat or checked in with his probation officer for three weeks. Yet there was nothing on the television about him which he had half expected. He hadn't contacted Marie and his children except by eye contact with Marie at Elliot Abbott's funeral. Rapier had warned him what would happen if he did and he wasn't going to take any chances.

Everything was set up in the cottage. There was plenty of duct tape, rope and a startling amount of ammo which concerned Morgan. Foy and Fisher wanted to go in heavy, and an array of guns were stacked ready. Foy had got his hands on some Glock 17 pistols with the barrels switched out for threaded barrels to fit a silencer along with big magazines for plenty of bullets. Morgan didn't like the look of the firepower, but Foy assured him it was necessary.

Glan Morgan was to make sure they had food for a few days. He didn't need to concern himself with the weapons. Foy and Fisher could handle them, which was just as well. Glan Morgan had never killed anything in his life and wasn't about to start now.

Glan hoped they wouldn't have to hold the children for too long. It was going to be a painful few days, but the reward would allow Morgan to live the life he had always wanted.

Chapter Forty

Jamie waited in the car for Claire while she checked in on Jason and Becky Keane. They had decided to have a night out themselves. With only three weeks to Christmas, they were looking forward to Jamie moving down permanently. They had agreed to meet Bonnie the following weekend, and if things went well then, Bonnie would spend Christmas with them in Fowey. They would be a family for the first time, and this would be their first Christmas together. Jamie thought it was a splendid idea.

Claire couldn't relax. The firearm officers had been with the Keane's for a week, and everything was quiet. Hutchens, Mac and Pearce had been keeping an eye on James Foy who was working in a discount tyre and brake centre in St Austell, but so far Foy appeared to be the perfect employee. He arrived on time, worked hard and then went straight home, occasionally popping into the pub on his way home. What they didn't know was that once Foy was home, and the police watching his place, he left through a back door to rendezvous with Morgan or Fisher.

DCS Butler wanted the team re-allocated. They were wasting their time. There was insufficient evidence to suggest the Keane's were in danger. All the police had was a hunch based on a note found in Glan Morgan's flat. They had other active cases that needed solving. When Butler informed Cornish of her decision, Cornish had stalked from her office and called the Chief Constable.

Chief Constable Falconbridge's hands were tied. Cornish listened and sighed as she rubbed at the tension, beginning to spread across her forehead. She was under attack from all sides.
'But surely you realise DCS Butler is trying to manipulate you so she can break the team apart?'

Butler had managed to persuade the Chief Constable that this was a wild goose chase and Falconbridge had to agree. They had a budget to work to and, with no other leads, to continue the firearm officers any longer at the Keane residence was a waste of resources.

Cornish argued to keep the Firearm officers until after the weekend. Falconbridge relented and agreed. When she told Butler, she opened her mouth to protest, but Falconbridge held up her agreement with Cornish. Cornish had seventy-two hours before the case was closed down.

Danielle Butler was looking forward to putting Cornish back in her box. The department needed fresh blood which not only looked and sounded the part but acted it too. If Butler had her way, Cornish would be gone soon. Butler needed somebody trustworthy to help her get to grips with the department and be her right-hand man. She wanted Cornish out.

Chief Constable Falconbridge had no intention of sacking or side-lining Cornish. She knew how to run her department, and Cornish was bloody good at her job. She wasn't going to give Butler the satisfaction of winning if she had a choice. While Butler might think her Chief Constable had no idea of what she was capable of, Cornish did.

Cornish was conscious that the next seventy-two hours were the most important of her career if she was to survive under DCS Butler.

As they drove away from Penpol, Jamie could hear the doubt in Claire's voice.

'You've done everything to help this family, Claire. You are one of the best DCI's there is. Don't let this DCS Butler push you around. I thought you loved your job?'

'I'll never be my own person as long as I'm living in DCS Butler's shadow. She hates me. She pours poison in the ears of anybody who will listen.'

They drove in silence for a few minutes while Claire assessed her relationship with Butler and her investigation. She was on the mark; she was sure of that. Her hunches had never let her down before. Butler was prepared to place everything on the line because of her petty jealousies and hate for Cornish.

Thankfully, hate was an emotion Cornish readily understood and could easily exploit.

Chapter Forty-One

Jason and Becky Keane were out, and Sienna and Lowenna were watching a film upstairs with Hilda. Downstairs the two police officers were in the kitchen. The alarm wasn't on and didn't need to be with all the protection. It was then Hilda heard a noise. She wasn't concerned with armed officers in the house.

All of a sudden footsteps and muffled voices could be heard on the stairs, and Hilda opened the bedroom door to see what was going on. They were at the far end of the hall, and Hilda stiffened as she saw the strangers wearing masks reach the top of the stairs. They were carrying guns, and she screamed in terror, but they had nowhere to hide. Hilda clutched the girls, who by this time were screaming, as the men wrenched them from Hilda who was begging the men not to hurt them. With a gun to her head, she was tied up and a piece of tape placed over her mouth.

The men picked up the girls and carried them down the stairs screaming. The girls wouldn't shut up, and Fisher slapped some tape on their mouths. Sienna and Lowenna were placed in cotton sacks and bundled into the waiting van which Foy had managed to get from work. They threw their weapons into the truck and moments later, they were gone. No one heard or saw them. Five minutes later, they were at the cottage, and the two bundles were carried quickly from the van inside.

'We had a slight problem,' Foy said to Morgan as soon as the children were locked in their room.

'What do you mean. How small?'
'There were two police officers in the house that you conveniently forgot to mention,' Foy said calmly but pissed. 'We had to get rid of them.'

'That wasn't what we agreed,' Glan retorted angrily. 'What exactly did you do?'
'Let's just say whoever was there is no longer a problem,' Fisher replied.

'Oh my God, you murdered them?'

'Had no choice, man,' said Foy.

Glan Morgan knew Rapier wasn't going to like it. How had he missed the police there? Glan Morgan felt a chill run down his back. There was no such thing as a free lunch, and this was going to cost Glan Morgan dearly. Foy and Fisher left Glan to deal with the kids. They weren't their problem now. Morgan was in charge of the cottage. Foy had to get back home before the police came knocking.

He was expecting an early wake-up call.

Chapter Forty-Two

When Jason and Becky Keane got home, it was well after midnight. The house was dark and eerily quiet. As Jason opened the front door, his hackles were up. Something was wrong. Switching the light on Jason called out. No one answered and then Becky shrieked as she saw the bloodstains on the wooden flooring leading up the stairs and off towards the kitchen. They followed the stains into the kitchen where the scene was one of total carnage. Becky screamed when she saw the dead bodies of the police officers. There was blood splattered everywhere, and the faceless corpses of the two officers slumped in their seats.

Jason was now running through the house and up the stairs shouting for Sienna and Lowenna. He was expecting to find them dead, everyone else was. He found Hilda bound and gagged and crying. As he ripped off the tape, she cried out that the girls had been snatched.

Cornish answered her mobile and sat bolt upright. Jane Falconbridge was the bearer of the bad news. Cornish's worst nightmare had come true. The two girls had been kidnapped.

When Cornish arrived at Tresco House, her whole team were there. DCS Butler had been informed by the Chief Constable Jane Falconbridge. Butler would be pissed that she had been passed over in the chain of command. Cornish didn't want to say I told you so.

Becky Keane was sobbing uncontrollably, and Cornish wanted a doctor to administer something to calm her down. They were all in shock and especially at the violence that had taken place. Jason tried to keep a cool head. They wanted their girls back. Were they already dead?

Cornish tried to manage the situation explaining that it would do the kidnappers no good to kill Sienna and Lowenna. Not if they expected to be paid. As Cornish left the on-call doctor with Jason and Becky Keane, she joined her team in the kitchen. Lucy Turner and Emma Bray were on the scene with the rest of SOCO. Everyone was wearing PPE suits as the area was assessed for usable prints and evidence. Turner informed Cornish that there were two distinct, sets of footprints at the scene and they had both been wearing gloves. Both officers never had a chance to use their guns. The kidnappers had the element of surprise and used silencers.

Cornish and Hutchens turned their attention to Hilda who was now sat in the lounge being consoled. She had only seen two men, and they were wearing masks and had been frightening. Cornish couldn't believe that her officers were dead, gunned down.

Jason and Becky were distraught, hysterical and Cornish desperately needed to find the children. With Jason, Becky and Hilda sobbing, Jason held his wife trying to console her, rocking her, as Becky's eyes looked wild and terrified. They wouldn't get much more from Hilda. She had been too terrified to notice any details. Jason wanted to kill whoever had done this.

'We'll get the girls back. I promise,' said Cornish praying that nothing went wrong. They would be expecting a call requesting the ransom. The problem was they had no money to bargain with. But the kidnappers didn't know that.

Cornish sat down next to Jason and Becky while Hutchens made the coffee. She had arranged for a family liaison officer to be with them. It was the least they could do to help them cope with grief and worry.

It was a long night as the bodies of the two young police officers were removed and sent over to the mortuary ready for Gilbert. Blue and white tape had closed off the kitchen section of the house which now resembled a war zone. The bullets had blown the brains and faces off the officers. The kitchen looked like a war zone as shots had ricocheted around the wall and units.

There were no sirens, and the blue lights flashed quietly in front of Tresco House. Cornish didn't want the press involved, and the official statement was that of an incident. The media could speculate all they wanted. The kidnappers were not to be alarmed. Anything said publicly could jeopardise the girl's lives. Cornish needed her team to act with extreme caution.

Chapter Forty-Three

Morgan left the girls to cry themselves to sleep. He didn't offer

them anything to drink, and he didn't want them to recognise

him. He switched on the early breakfast news. Nothing was being

said about the shooting in Penpol. Morgan decided to ring

Rapier. He knew he would be pissed off to get a call, but he

thought he should know exactly what went down.

Rapier answered on the third ring.

'If anything gets out about the kidnapping to the press, then we

are all dead. You need to make sure that doesn't happen. It's time

for you to earn that money, Morgan. Remember what will happen

else.'

Morgan didn't like Rapier's tone, but he had no choice. He didn't

want anybody else killed. Morgan checked on the girls, they were

asleep and still securely tied up. Using his burner mobile, he

called the police line. In less than a few minutes, Cornish was alerted to the message. Falconbridge had made it clear no one slipped up.

Miles Fisher had slunk back into his hole while James Foy heard of an incident in Penpol on the 9 am news. No further details were being given out, and the press weren't making waves. Foy hadn't expected the two police officers to be there. Their murder was definitely a problem. He needed his money, but in the meantime, he had to remain calm.

Chapter Forty-Four

Charles Rapier was enjoying his holiday with his wife. He knew what was happening back home. What he hadn't expected were Morgan's accomplices to blow the brains out of two police officers. That complicated things. But it was Morgan's problem, not his. He had an alibi for the time of the murders and the kidnapping of Jason and Becky Keane's daughters.

Rapier had told Morgan to wait a few days before contacting the police. Let the Keane's and the police sweat. He wanted Jason and Becky Keane in a state of panic. If they were, then they would be more likely to pay up the ransom, and faster. He didn't consider for one moment that they didn't have the money. If they didn't pay then Morgan was to kill the two little girls.

There was no mention of a kidnapping in the local papers and news, and Rapier knew Morgan had contacted the police and warned them not to say anything to the press. For the moment they were doing just that.

Rapier was cross about the way Morgan had handled the kidnapping, but he held his tongue. All three of them were loose cannons potentially. He was sure that only Glan Morgan knew his identity. Otherwise, Morgan knew Rapier would kill him.

Morgan was in charge of the girls at the cottage, and he hoped it stayed that way. He didn't want Foy and Fisher hurting their valuable prizes and he wasn't sure their babysitting skills were reliable. Rapier had told Morgan that he didn't want Foy and Fisher turning up at the cottage and risking any nosey neighbours seeing too much coming and going. Morgan was to stay with the girls and protect them until the ransom was paid.

Rapier had made it his business to find out about Foy and Fisher once he knew they were involved. He recognised Foy from the day that Morgan was released. And he had been correct in his assessment that Morgan would contact Foy, he had been banking on that. But Fisher was something else. He had been chosen by Foy. Rapier didn't want Foy and Fisher getting out of control.

They needed to be patient if they wanted their share and not

hotheads. They had a plan, and they all just had to stick to it.

Rapier told Morgan to sit tight until it was time.

Chapter Forty-Five

Gary Gilbert had the unpleasant task of carrying out the post-mortem on the two police officers. This was now very personal. He knew the two young officers which made his task harder. Gilbert couldn't imagine how the families were coping. Neither had been married, but the parents had lost their sons. It didn't seem right to lose a child at whatever age.

Cornish and Pearce watched the post-mortem through the glass screen. There were already too many around the stainless steel tables. Both bodies were there so that Gilbert could relay precisely what happened.

Cornish had seen her fair share of post-mortems in the past. She had become desensitised over the years to the mortuary environment, unlike Pearce. Gilbert started at the top.

Pearce could feel his shirt clinging to his back. No matter how many examinations he had attended, he always wanted to throw up. No matter what he ate, or didn't eat, the result was still the same. You either had the stomach for this sort of thing or not. Pearce didn't.

The clothing from both bodies had been removed and bagged and tagged.

Gilbert had completed the standard post-mortem procedures already by the time Cornish and Pearce had arrived. As far as Cornish was concerned, they had already established the cause of death, and she wasn't expecting there to be any more surprises. The whole procedure of removing organs and in most cases, returning them back to the body seemed unnecessary. Still, the rules were in place to ensure consistency and fair practice.

Gilbert explained his findings to Cornish and Pearce on how the two men met their tragic end. There was never a nice way to explain how lives were ended, especially when it had been a violent death.

'Victim A, Constable Shelley was killed by a Glock 17 pistol. Two bullets hit him directly in the back of the head exiting out the front. The other four rounds hit the victim in the torso. The victim had his back to the shooter, and the range would suggest that the shooters opened fire as they entered the room. As you can see, most of his facial features have been destroyed.

Victim B, Constable Wakefield was killed by a second Glock 17 pistol, but this time the bullets entered the front of his face exiting the back of the head. Two shots hit his chest. He was slightly protected by Constable Shelley whose body position somewhat shielded him from further impact. Again, there isn't much left of the police officers facial features.

Fragments of brain, bones and blood were sprayed and splattered over all the surfaces of the area, the floor, walls. And ceilings as well as all the furniture. Both officers had been sitting down at the time and it appears they were taken by complete surprise. Their guns were still in their holsters, and I suspect the shooters used a silencer.

Gilbert paused, catching his breath.

'Such a shame to die so young with their whole lives ahead of them.'

Cornish and Pearce stepped out of the hospital and breathed in the fresh air to get rid of the smell of death.

Pearce glanced over at his boss.

'It's a hell of a business, death.'

Cornish filed away the report to the back of her mind. No one deserved to die like that, and she intended to catch the killers and bring them to justice.

Chapter Forty-Six

Glan Morgan sat in the cottage staring at the TV. He was transfixed hoping that this nightmare would soon be over. All he wanted was his money and to get far away. The only reason he was doing this was to save his ex-wife and his children. With the death of the two police officers, Morgan knew there was no way out for him. He was done for.

Morgan tried to think of Jason and Becky Keane and what they must be going through. He desperately wanted this to turn out all right in the end. He wanted the two little girls reunited with their parents. He was sure the Keane's would pay the ransom. But Glan Morgan knew he had no choice but to see it through to the end. He didn't trust Rapier, and after what had happened at the Keane's home, he didn't trust Foy and Fisher. Glan Morgan didn't want anything worse to happen than already had.

Glan Morgan had no idea what was going on outside the cottage. He hadn't stepped out for a couple of days. And all he had to do now was make the phone call to Jason and Becky Keane so the ransom could be paid.

Chapter Forty-Seven

DS Pearce and DC Mac knocked on the council house door. They were there to search the premises. Foy casually opened the door and stepped aside. He knew the routine. The police officers wouldn't find anything incriminating.

The officers spent two hours going through Foy's personal items with a fine-tooth comb. There was nothing there. No papers or articles or any hint of wrongdoing. Foy by all accounts was clean. Only Pearce and Mac doubted that was the case.

Foy was a model citizen. He turned up for work on time, got on with the job in hand and left promptly. His neighbours weren't aware of anything and had no idea he had recently been released from prison. They all assumed he had moved down to Cornwall looking for a fresh start which was the story he gave to anyone that asked.

Pearce and Mac left Foy to place his things back in order and called Cornish with the news.

Foy watched the two officers leave and smiled. Prison had taught him many things.

Chapter Forty-Eight

Cornish and her team worked around the clock. There was someone present with Jason and Becky Keane all the time. The telephone lines and their mobile phones were being monitored, and Cornish anticipated that it wouldn't be too long before the kidnappers called. There was no question in her mind that they would call. Armed police officers were on alert, and Cornish wanted to be ready for anything. DCS Butler had turned up and spoken to Jason and Becky Keane, but it was obvious to all that Cornish was running the show.

Becky Keane looked like a ghost. She wasn't holding up well, and the doctor had given her some medication to help her cope. She felt dead inside. She never wanted to see the kitchen again, and she would certainly never forget.

Jason just wanted the whole episode over, but Cornish was concerned because she knew they didn't have the money to meet the kidnappers' demands. It was all she could think of when she discussed it with Jason Keane. She knew he would have told her if he had any other funds, he could get his hands on. Cornish had to ask all the same.

Jason Keane felt sorry for the police officers killed protecting his family. Indirectly, he felt responsible for their deaths. Cornish tried to reassure him that this was what they did, protecting the public. It was a risk, and sometimes lives were lost. Most of the time, things turned out fine, but this wasn't one of them.

The question that had been on everyone's lips was what was going to happen when the ransom demand was made.

'What am I going to do when they ask for money?'

Cornish had been thinking about it non-stop. She was hoping that they would be able to trace the call and move in quickly. Any delay could result in further bloodshed, especially when the kidnappers realised there was no money. They needed to find

Sienna and Lowenna fast. Cornish didn't want to think the worst, that they may not be able to trace the call.

Cornish instructed Mac, Pearce and Hutchens to check out the neighbourhood. Walking around the local houses might give them a lead. Cornish doubted the kidnappers had driven too far; they would be somewhere nearby holding up. They were now playing a waiting game.

Becky Keane looked worse the longer it went on. Every time the phone rang, everyone jumped. Jason Keane was holding up better than his wife. Becky slept in her clothes in the girl's rooms. She didn't care that her home was full of police, all she cared about was getting her children home.

Cornish watched Jason and Becky Keane coping in their different ways. Jason liked to be kept informed and in the loop whereas, Becky withdrew into herself. Cornish prayed the wait would be over soon.

And prayed that Sienna and Lowenna were still alive.

Chapter Forty-Nine

Glan Morgan removed the tape from the girl's mouths so they could eat and drink. They needed to take in some fluids. Neither looked great, and Glan Morgan was concerned.

'I recognise you,' Sienna whispered.

Glan hadn't expected the older girl to recognise him so quickly. She was astute. He had forgotten to mask up. Not that it mattered anymore. His life was over.

Glan spoke gently as he would have to his own children. He didn't want them getting hysterical. Both girls needed the bathroom and Glan took them one at a time. Sienna looked awkward for a minute, and Glan then noticed that both girls had wet themselves and not said anything. There was nothing he could do, he had no spare clothes, so he just covered them with a blanket each, replaced the tape and ties and left them in the locked room.

Glan Morgan was not enjoying this part of the plan. He hadn't envisaged it would be like this. The girls were terrified, afraid and in shock. He tried to placate them and offer them regular drinks and biscuits, but they were completely distraught by what had happened.

Sienna spoke up when her tape was removed.

'Are you going to kill us?'

She looked so small and frightened, and all Glan wanted to do was hug them, but he couldn't. He had done this to them, caused all this, and they were terrified he was going to kill them.

'No, I'm not. You are both going home in a few days once your mum and dad have paid the ransom.'

'They haven't got any money,' Sienna answered.

'How do you know?' asked Glan.

'I heard them talking. We are broke, and mummy and daddy are worried.'

Glan Morgan looked worried as he closed the door and listened to the sobs. He didn't like this and listening to them made him feel sick. If what Sienna had said was true then this would end badly for everyone.

Foy and Fisher arrived to check on Glan Morgan and his charges. Morgan didn't say anything about the chat with Sienna. They were going to make the ransom demand, and Glan brought up the possibility that Jason and Becky Keane might refuse to pay.
'If they don't pay up then I say we get rid of the girls. Dump them and get the fuck out,' said Foy.
Fisher agreed. The girls could identify all three of them.
Glan Morgan suddenly realised that there was never any intention of releasing the girls. Even if the ransom was paid. Glan Morgan had every right to be profoundly worried.

Morgan made the call as agreed. Foy and Fisher hanging on his every word. Cornish, Butler and Jane Falconbridge listened to the demands. The police were recording and trying to trace the call. Both girls spoke, and Becky Keane collapsed as she heard her daughter's voices and pleas.

The kidnapper sounded intelligent and educated. He was polite and oddly gentle in his tone. And calm. If their demands weren't met, then the girls would be killed. Becky Keane fainted.

They had seventy-two hours to pay the ransom, and they would be given the account details for the money. Glan Morgan knew the money would be moved instantly it hit that account and transported through the ether. And onto its eventual untraceable final destination in incredibly quick time.

The police would never be able to trace the money, and it would vanish into thin air. The problem was if Sienna was telling the truth and there was no money.

Glan Morgan ended the call, and Cornish looked at the IT expert who was shaking his head. Glan Morgan had cut off too soon and used a burner phone. They couldn't trace the call. They had seventy-two hours, but it might as well have been twenty-four or one hundred and twenty hours. It didn't matter.

They had no money to pay the ransom.

Chapter Fifty

Glan Morgan was getting nervous. Foy and Fisher were getting ever more anxious to end this and get their money. They didn't care about the girls. They would be dead soon, anyway.

Glan Morgan made the second call to Jason and Becky Keane. Time was running out, and this time he wanted to know if they had the money ready to pay the ransom. He sounded impatient on the phone as Cornish listened in. Glan Morgan gave Jason Keane the payment details for the ransom, and Jason wrote down the information. Hope was dwindling by the hour as Jason and Becky Keane couldn't pay the demands.

'It's going to take me longer than that to access the money,' replied Jason trying not to let panic creep into his voice. Cornish had instructed him to ask for more time. They were fighting for Sienna and Lowenna's lives.

'Time is running out,' Morgan said firmly. 'My associates will not wait past the deadline.'

Glan Morgan rang off. Foy and Fisher would not wait much longer, Morgan knew that. Foy had now left his house and Fisher his bedsit, and they were going nowhere without their money. 'If the money isn't paid on time, the girls are dead, and we're out of here,' Foy barked.

Foy and Fisher's moods were getting darker. They were fed up waiting, and there was no beer in the cottage. Glan had wanted everyone to maintain a clear, cool head, but it was obvious that if he didn't do something, then the girls would be hurt. Glan Morgan offered to walk to the local shop to pick some up.

Glan bought what tins they had in the little shop and started to walk back to the cottage. He knew they were running out of time, and the ransom was looking like a lost cause. He had to let the girls go before Foy and Fisher killed them. He had no choice. He would do the same for his children. He knew what he had to do.

Glan Morgan dialled the Keane's home number, and when Jason Keane picked up, he asked to speak to the officer in charge. He knew the police would be there or on the line. With the murder of two police officers and kidnap, it was standard procedure.

DCI Cornish answered the call.

'This is DCI Cornish,' Claire answered tersely.

'You have to get the girls out of here. There are three of us here, including me. If I don't do what I'm told, my children will be killed.'

Glan Morgan had thought carefully about what he would say when the time came. He was an accomplice, but he had been forced to kidnap the Keane' daughters to save his children's lives. What choice did he have?

Jason and Becky Keane were terrified as they listened in on the conversation.

'Morgan is that you?' asked Cornish.

Glan Morgan didn't confirm or deny. He had more important things to do. He couldn't live with himself if the two girls were killed. Glan gave Cornish the address where he was holding the girls and described the layout of the property. He told Cornish that the girls were safe so far. Jason and Becky Keane breathed a sigh of relief at hearing the news. But this wasn't over yet, and Cornish couldn't afford to get complacent. There was plenty that could go wrong between now and getting Sienna and Lowenna back. The call was being recorded, and Cornish asked the question.

'Is Charles Rapier behind this?'

Glan Morgan hesitated for a moment before answering.

'Yes, he is, but if he finds out I've said anything, then he will kill my children. I'm a dead man anyway.'

Glan Morgan knew he couldn't hide forever. Rapier would soon find him and kill him.

'I'm doing this for the two girls and my children. I'm sorry,' replied Morgan. And with that, he hung up and strolled back to the cottage contemplating his last few hours of freedom. He would be back behind bars soon enough. For once in his life, he had done the right thing, and it felt good.

'What the fuck took you so long?' Foy asked, but he mellowed when Morgan handed him a beer.

Morgan checked on the girls. They were exhausted and sound asleep. Hopefully, the next time they rose would be to their freedom thought Glan. He just hoped that would be soon before Foy and Fisher decided to take matters into their own hands.

Chapter Fifty-One

Cornish looked at her team who were waiting for her response. Jason and Becky Keane were clinging to each other, hoping that the end was near. Their girls were still alive, but for how much longer no one knew.

'They are just down the road, within earshot of home,' Cornish said.

It was the break they needed, and the only hope of getting the girls now was to act swiftly. Foy and Fisher wouldn't hang on once they realised the ransom would not be paid. Glan Morgan had been clear on that point.

Cornish called Butler and Falconbridge. She needed the armed response section. They were going to require armed officers to storm the cottage and bring out the girls. Everything had to be executed with precision timing if they were going to avoid any fatalities.

The next morning, early, all the armed officers were assembled at Tresco House. Cornish and her team had firearms. This would be the first time in as many years that Cornish had ever felt the need to carry a weapon. The Keane's hadn't heard from the kidnappers since yesterday. They knew the risks. Cornish had explained at length what would happen. They had no choice if they wanted to see their daughters again. There was no money to bargain with, and Cornish didn't want to say that even if they had the money, the girls would most certainly be killed.

The liaison officer would stay with Jason and Becky Keane. Cornish and her team would take up their positions at the address given by Morgan.

In the cottage, Morgan had no idea when the police would turn up. Foy and Fisher were getting restless and at each other's throats. Morgan called Rapier as arranged. He told him there was no ransom money, the Keane's didn't have the funds. Rapier didn't believe him. Morgan didn't let on to Foy and Fisher they wouldn't get paid. That would have accelerated the girl's deaths.

At the end of the small lane leading to the cottage, Cornish and her team of armed officers were preparing. The road, in and out of the hamlet, was blocked. The residents had been ordered to stay inside their homes. Cornish was in charge of the operation. She knew the girls were in a back room of the cottage. She had no way now of contacting Glan Morgan to warn him they were coming in. It was now or never.

Glan Morgan had picked the perfect place to hide-out. The back garden was fully enclosed. Anyone entering the property would be visible from the front. They would be sitting targets to Foy and Fisher. It was damn near impossible to quietly sneak in without being spotted. But that was what they had to do to get the girls out.

'My team are walking into a firefight,' the firearms officer in charge of his team said unhappily to Cornish. 'Our only hope is the element of surprise. Once the kidnappers are awake, the risk will be too great. And we don't have any more time.'

Cornish had left Jason and Becky Keane with the hope and impression that this would soon be over. But Cornish knew that wasn't the case. Kidnappings often went wrong and especially at the end. Things were not looking good from where Cornish and her team were standing. But they had no choice. This was a matter of life or death.

'There has to be a way to get the girls out alive,' was all Pearce said.

'We can't control it all. Not to mention luck and fate and what Foy and Fisher do when we storm the cottage. We just have to hope they back down or we take them down quickly. We have one advantage, and that's Morgan. Hopefully, he can keep the girls safe, and no one gets hurt,' replied Cornish worried that this could all blow up in their face.

Still, that was a big ask and Cornish knew that. It was the luck of the draw. Any perfect plan could go awry at the last minute. It only took one person to open fire at the wrong moment, and then all hell would be let loose.

Chapter Fifty-Two

Jason and Becky Keane sat by the phone, waiting to hear that their girls were safe. The police had left in the early hours to get set up and have the element of surprise.

Outside the cottage, Cornish and her team were in position. The place was in darkness, and the police were using infrared to check out the house. Cornish hoped they were all still asleep inside. Officers had slowly crept towards the cottage and managed to hide in the bushes closest to the property. They would offer some protection and cover to those entering the building.

At the exact moment, officers moved to the side and back of the cottage. There were French doors at the back of the house that would lead them through the lounge towards the bedrooms. Cornish hoped all the kidnappers were asleep in the bedrooms and not in the lounge. There was a small window in the girl's bedroom, but it wouldn't make a quick getaway having to scramble through. Fully armed with semi-automatic Glock 17 pistols, the armed officers silently made their way.

Glan Morgan slept in the room nearest to the girls while Foy and Fisher shared the twin-bedded room. Morgan wanted to be near the girls when the police made their move. His primal instinct told him to stay awake. Glan Morgan wasn't sure what spooked him first, whether it was a rustle of movement or his heightened senses. It was still dark outside as something stirred. He looked out of the window of his bedroom. The sky was more charcoal than inky, and the sun would be up shortly. He couldn't see anything, and he hoped the police were out there. He knew that Foy and Fisher were set to kill the girls if the ransom wasn't paid, and time was nearly up.

Glan Morgan no longer cared for his safety. He was standing at the window when he thought he heard a sound. He strained to look beyond the darkness when a small stone hit his window. That was the signal. Glan crept into the girl's bedroom and gently shook Sienna and Lowenna whispering to be very quiet. He removed their tape and untied the rope and held their hands. They realised that Glan Morgan was going to help them escape. They silently walked out of the bedroom and into the lounge hoping that none of the old floorboards creaked. Two armed officers were waiting by the French doors to take the girls away from the danger. Glan Morgan opened the doors, and four hands reached out and grabbed Sienna and Lowenna and ran with such speed and force it took their breath away. As they vanished into the darkness, Glan Morgan turned to go back to his bedroom when Foy came out of the bedroom to go to the bathroom. Foy gave Morgan a start before saying, 'You're up early. Have you checked the girls?'

Morgan was about to reply when Foy noticed something move past the window.

'What's wrong said Morgan,' looking concerned.

'I'm not sure,' replied Foy as he shouted to Fisher to get his sorry ass out of bed and grab the guns.

There was no way Morgan could warn the police outside that Foy and Fisher had heard something. Foy signalled to Fisher to watch the front of the house, and as he did, Fisher saw the two officers running down the path carrying something in their arms. Foy ran into the girl's room.

'They've gone. The girls aren't here.' Foy turned to Morgan. 'What the fuck have you done?'
Foy slammed Morgan against the wall with his gun held to his head and looked Glan Morgan dead in the eye.
'You called the police, didn't you. You fucking ratted us out. You fucked me out of my money.' Foy was blind with anger.

'They don't have the money,' Morgan said.

'What the fuck do you know?' Foy said as he turned to look down the drive to see the police advancing towards the cottage.

Foy and Fisher smashed the windows and opened fire. The police responded. The girls were safe, and now Cornish wanted to bring all three kidnappers in alive.

Foy and Fisher emptied their guns as they repeatedly fired at the armed response officers. Neither side was backing down. Morgan crouched in the bedroom covering his ears as the sound of ammunition being emptied was deafening. The siege lasted an hour as Foy and Fisher held out until the tear gas canisters were thrown into the cottage. Foy wasn't going back to prison for anyone. Fisher made a dash for the bushes but was gunned down as he took one of the armed officers with him. Foy retreated into the bedroom where Morgan was hiding.

Foy looked at Morgan aiming the gun, 'I want what's mine,' and fired two shots before the armed officers grappled him to the ground and cuffed him.

Cornish walked into the cottage to survey the scene. Glan Morgan was dead, gunned down by Foy. Fisher's body lay on the ground outside. She saw the room the girls had been held in and the array of guns and ammunition that Foy and Fisher had and were prepared to use. The house had been rented in Glan Morgan's name. As Foy was carted away, Cornish thought of the lives wasted. She had lost one armed officer in the battle who had a family. Cornish would have to tell his family.

Cornish met Butler on the pathway walking towards the cottage. There was a short pause before Cornish informed Butler that Glan Morgan was dead. Butler smiled thinly commenting, 'it was the least he deserved.'
Cornish didn't respond.

The kidnapping was over but not without a cost to other families. And Marie Abbott would need to be told that her ex-husband and father to her children was dead.

Turner and Bray and the rest of the SOCO team would spend the next few hours piecing together the siege and removing the bodies. A couple of the CSIs were brushing the undergrowth in the perimeter around Miles Fisher's body. Gilbert would be kept busy with the post-mortems, but it was a mere formality. The police tried to reassure the neighbours, and Cornish gave strict instructions to say nothing to the press. This was a private family matter.

Too many people had lost their lives, and Cornish wanted to bring the real villain to justice. Men had died because of Charles Rapier, and if they hadn't died, then two innocent girls would have been killed.

Glan Morgan had made a difference in the end. He had saved Sienna and Lowenna.

Chapter Fifty-Three

Jason and Becky cried with relief when Sienna and Lowenna were safe and home. They couldn't say anything except clutch their daughters who they thought they might never see alive again. The ambulance was there waiting to take the girls to Royal Cornwall Hospital in Treliske to get them checked over after their ordeal. It would take more than a check-up to heal their wounds. The whole family had been affected. The trauma of the kidnapping still had a quality of unreality to it, for all of them.

Cornish knew it would take time to heal their mental wounds. Jason and Becky Keane couldn't thank Cornish and her team enough for what they had done. They felt awful for the armed police officer who had been killed saving their daughters, and no words of thanks would be enough. Jason asked Cornish to let them know when the funeral was as they wanted to pay their respects. Cornish assured them she would. She intended to keep in touch with them over the coming weeks to ensure they were alright and coping with the aftermath. Her investigations were not yet over. They hadn't caught Elliot Abbott's murderer, and that was still ongoing, but it was safe to say the Keane's were no longer suspects.

The news emerged of the kidnapping in Penpol. Cornish was keen to keep the two incidents separate. Danielle Butler was seething, having listened to the statement given by Cornish to the press. They had lapped up the news and Cornish, once again, was the hero of the hour. Butler's eyes swept over Cornish, and at that moment, Butler hated Cornish more than ever.

Falconbridge had watched the news bulletin from her office observing the look between the two women. This wasn't over.

Chapter Fifty-Four

Charles Rapier landed in the UK expecting to resume a normal life. He hadn't expected to be greeted by DCI Cornish and DS Pearce. His wife slapped him before the police took him away. He had plenty of questions to answer back at the police headquarters.

James Foy was already in custody. Cornish questioned Foy who held out for several hours before admitting he had placed the car bomb at Judge Mercers. The opportunity was too good to miss. Foy was going back to prison for a long time. The evidence against Foy for the kidnapping was enough to get a long sentence and then there was the murder of Glan Morgan. James Foy would never see the light of day again.

Still, Cornish wanted confirmation that Rapier was at the helm. Foy didn't know who had been in charge. Only Glan Morgan had that information, and he was dead. The police needed hard evidence. Cornish sent Pearce and Hutchens and Mac to Rapier's home.

Rapier was one sick bastard. He had a file on Jason Keane going back years before they were in business together. Magazines and newspaper articles and pictures of the girls at school. Rapier was fascinated, by Jason Keane, bordering on obsession. Cornish realised that once she had seen the information.

The other files were on Glan Morgan and his ex-wife, Marie Abbott and their children. Then there were files on Mr Smith and Maxwell Abbott whom Rapier had been in business with. He was working his way through those he held responsible for the loss of his money.

Charles Rapier sat in the interview room in Truro. His solicitor sat beside him as he was read his rights by Cornish.

'You are under arrest on suspicion of the kidnapping of Sienna and Lowenna Keane. We would also like to question you regarding the recent murder of Elliot Abbott. You do not have to say anything, but it may harm your defence if you do not mention when questioned something which you later rely on in court. Anything you do say may be given in evidence.

You understand your rights?'

'Yes, I understand.'

The mandated audio recording was turned on for the interview. Cornish concentrated on probing the suspect's account of events which she would later compare with the information collated. From the start, Charles Rapier denied he had anything to do with kidnapping the two girls. Prison was the last place Rapier was going. He claimed Glan Morgan had approached him with the plan. Morgan had been desperate for cash. Cornish let him carry on with his tale until she could stand no more. Presenting the evidence found in Rapiers concealed safe, opened by his wife, Charles Rapier's cheerful smile faded, leaving in its place a cold, blank expression. *That bitch.*

There was no reply from Rapier.

Cornish, along with Pearce, sat opposite Rapier and his solicitor. They looked uncomfortable as Cornish preceded to go through the breakdown of events and the dates and where Rapier was at the time.

The questioning had been going on for hours, several coffee breaks had been taken, and their suspect was steadfast in his refusal to talk. Eventually, tiredness appeared to get the better of Rapier, and his tune changed. It would still be his word against a dead man's.

'I admit I was angry and pissed off. Losing a lot of money tends to do that. But I didn't kidnap those two little girls, and I most certainly didn't murder Elliot Abbott.'

'But, Mr Rapier, you did know about the plot to kidnap the Keane children. You orchestrated the plan?'

Charles Rapier made no response.

'That makes you an accessory to kidnap.'

Still nothing.

Rapiers eyes shifted between the two police officers. His expression changed from resolute non-disclosure to concern. He eventually said, 'How'd you mean? I wasn't even here?'

'We have enough evidence to place you in the frame, Mr Rapier and send you away for a long time.'

Despite the threat of being charged with kidnapping, Rapier still seemed reluctant to answer, and instead, exchanged panicked glances between the two detectives before regaining some composure.

'I'm afraid that would be quite impossible, DCI Cornish. I have friends in high places that won't want me behind bars.'

It was evident from the stricken look on Rapier's face that he'd said something he hadn't intended to.

This interview was over. DCI Cornish switched off the recording. Colour surged into her face, and with a furious snarl, she instructed Charles Rapier to be taken to the police holding cell. With a heavy sigh, Cornish knew that the evidence found in Charles Rapier's safe might not be enough to put him behind bars. There was no DNA to tie him to the girls or Glan Morgan nor for that matter Elliot Abbott. However, Cornish was sure he hadn't murdered Elliot Abbott. CPS would make the call on the kidnap charge.

Cornish broached her concerns to DCS Butler.

'I'm sorry, but I must agree with the CPS. Without a more specific link between Glan Morgan and the two Girls kidnapped, the CPS is unlikely to bring the case to trial.'

Cornish turned to DCS Butler with angry eyes.

'You've got to be kidding. Rapier was behind the whole plan.'

'It may look that way from the documents found in Charles Rapier's home, but that's not a reason to convict him,' replied Butler. 'There's reasonable doubt given his alibi.'

Cornish squirmed, unable to believe what she was hearing. Danielle Butler just smiled. For once DCI Cornish wouldn't get her man and wouldn't be the hero of the press. Without a signed confession, Charles Rapier would walk free. Butler signed the paperwork to release him. She had made the decision to override Cornish.

Charles Rapier emerged from the police station. His eyes swept over Cornish, and something passed between them. The knowledge that Cornish had really seen him for what he was and yet had been forced to let him walk free.

Cornish had lost this battle.

Chapter Fifty-Five

DCS Butler picked up her home phone, she had been expecting the call. Danielle Butler had enjoyed putting Cornish in her place. She revelled in power she now had. The feeling was intoxicating.

Danielle Butler's voice melted like warm honey as she listened to the gratitude from Charles Rapier.

'Everything's fine,' she told him.

Danielle Butler was all he could see, all he wanted.

'What do you have planned this evening?'

Danielle Butler gently let Charles Rapier down. It wouldn't bode well to let him know he wasn't her sort. She needed him for his connections and nothing else. Charles Rapier had to be played carefully like the strings on a harp.

When she put the phone down, Danielle Butler realised it was not too late for her to change her mind, if she really wanted to. There were no second chances in life. Danielle had chosen her path. Her black eyes were filled with hate for one person, Claire Cornish. Butler's lips twisted into an ugly smile before she whispered, 'I'm watching you. There's nowhere to hide. Jamie Nance will soon be mine.'

Danielle Butler sipped her wine, looking out at the lights twinkling in the dark over Fowey. She was in rented accommodation for the moment, and Fowey suited her needs perfectly. She considered it would be a beautiful place to buy a home with Jamie.

As she basked in the warmth of the log-burner crackling, she made her plans.

Chapter Fifty-Six

Cornish kept to her word and checked in on Jason and Becky Keane after a few days. When Jason opened the door, he knew instantly that there was something wrong.

The industrial cleaning company were tearing Jason and Becky Keane's kitchen apart. Everything was being taken out and replaced right down to the flooring and the Silestone kitchen tops. They couldn't bear to look at it until it was replaced entirely and all trace of what had happened that night had been erased. There would be no visible evidence of what had taken place there when the two police officers were killed, and the girls kidnapped. But they would carry the mental scare forever.

Jason had mentioned to DCI Cornish that they had been so looking forward to their first Christmas in their new home, but now they had decided to go away. With the kitchen being ripped out and the whole placed redecorated they would start afresh in the new year. Cornish thought that was a sensible idea given the recent events.

Cornish had no further information on Elliot Abbott's killer, but the police were still following up leads. With the kidnapping taking priority, the police had been stretched.

Cornish had kept the most critical information until last, she was the bearer of bad news. Charles Rapier had been released. There was insufficient evidence to bring him to trial. As the words sunk in, all the memories of the last week flashed through Jason and Becky's minds. They would never get over what had happened to their family. They would eventually learn to deal with it and cope, but it would always be somewhere at the back of their minds. Sienna and Lowenna would need help for many months and years to come.

Cornish stood watching the family, and she wondered how long it would be before they laughed again.

Pearce had been waiting in the VW for Cornish. She had the task of imparting the news to Jason and Becky Keane, and he could only imagine how the conversation went. And by the look of his boss's face, not well.

Pearce sighed. He didn't know how the Keane's were coping so well. 'Even the most non-violent of people can be tested to their limits,' Pearce said, softly.

Thirty minutes later, Cornish and Pearce arrived at Callum Roberts home. It was Cornish's vocation to seek justice, and she would not rest until Elliot Abbott's murderer was caught and behind bars.

When they reached Robert's front door, they were greeted by Hutchens and Mac. In her hand, Cornish held a search warrant. There was nobody home as they entered the house and commenced their search.

It was a watershed moment when they found what they were looking for. Cornish and her team watched the copy back at the office. The killer was clearly seen in action. The scene was reconstructed in front of their eyes as the knife was plunged into Elliot Abbott's back. The night vision IR, infrared, enabled a clear HDR, high dynamic range, picture. There was no mistaking the murderer.

Callum Roberts wasn't at Holland House or at home. It was his day off. Cornish was concerned. If Callum Roberts wanted money in return for the film, then he was meeting the killer who had already struck once. In her experience, the killer would be most likely to kill him. Get rid of any loose ends.

Neither Cornish nor Pearce could even dare to think about what might be about to happen.

Callum Roberts needed to be warned.

Callum Roberts answered his mobile. If Cornish could have seen his face, she would have seen his displeasure at receiving a call from the police. He was on the verge of changing his life, for the better.

'DCI Cornish, what can I do for you today?'

Cornish had the fleeting impression that he was busy. That was fair enough except she was busy working, saving his life.

'Mr Roberts, we entered your property and found what you have been hiding. Under the circumstances, you are in danger if you are meeting that person hoping to get paid. But, of course, that will be your call to make. Where are you?'

Callum Roberts gave a slight smile, he wasn't worried. He'd come prepared.

'We need to have a chat soon, Mr Roberts. This can't wait. Tell me where you are?'

'If you must know I'm sitting in Boscawen Park.' *Waiting for my money.*

Stay exactly where you are. We are on our way,' instructed Cornish.

Cornish and Pearce quickly drove to the park. Cornish guessed what Callum Roberts was up to. She feared they would be too late. They parked Cornish's VW in the car park and scanned the area for Roberts. Pearce recognised him first. He was sitting on a bench and appeared to be watching the football match. As Cornish and Pearce walked up to the seat, they noticed the red stain on his shirt. With lightning speed, they reached Callum Roberts body. He was already dead.

Cornish made the call, and Pearce kept the sightseers away. 'It's not our job,' Pearce was about to finish his sentence when Cornish interrupted.

'Our job is to protect,' Cornish said. 'We failed.'

'Only because Callum Roberts wouldn't listen,' piped up Pearce. 'Don't beat yourself up. He had a choice.'

Turner and Bray turned up along with the ambulance to take

Callum Roberts to Gilbert.

Cornish turned to Pearce.

'Come on, let's go and pick up our killer. It's time to end this.'

Chapter Fifty-Seven

Cornish and Pearce heard the footsteps approaching. As the front door opened, Cornish didn't waste any time on pleasantries but came straight to the point.

'Marie Abbott, you are under arrest on suspicion of the murder of Elliot Abbott and Callum Roberts. You do not have to say anything, but it may harm your defence if you do not mention when questioned something which you later rely on in court. Anything you do say may be given in evidence.

You understand your rights?'

'Yes, I understand.'

Marie Abbott seemed rooted to the spot as the reality of her situation set in. She needed to arrange for her parents to collect the children from school and look after them. The game was up.

Marie Abbott caved in. She knew when she was beaten. She would have got away with it had Callum Roberts not recorded the whole murder. Marie Abbott suspected the life assurance claim would now be invalidated. That hadn't been her primary reason for wanting Elliot dead. He was a monster and had to be stopped. Her children would be parentless. First, their father and now their mother. It would fall to her parents to raise her children.

Cornish sighed inwardly; 'for the love of money is the root of all evil.' Lives had been lost because of greed and desire. Elliot Abbott had refused to leave quietly and been killed. He had failed to face his own crimes and demons, and in some way, Cornish felt the law was twisted. Who were the real victims in all this?

The press would look at this as a victory. Two murders solved. Two for the price of one. It would be a big night for the news desk.

It had been a long week. The team had been busy all year as each crime rolled into the next one.

Chief Constable Falconbridge congratulated Cornish on a great result, and DCS Butler was forced to address the press extolling the virtues of her DCI and the team. Cornish knew how much making that statement had peeved Butler. Butler gave no indication that she harboured a grudge against Cornish. Cornish watched the speech with an unreadable expression that could have signified contempt. With a tight smile. She was due a well-earned weekend off. And so were her team. She intended to make sure she called the shots from now on.

Jane Falconbridge sat back at her desk and watched DCS Butler address her audience. She would have preferred to see Cornish as the new superintendent, but since she had turned down the job, she'd have to make do with Butler.

And the sooner Cornish came to terms with that, the better.

Chapter Fifty-Eight

Of all the times to have a reunion with their daughter Claire and Jamie had to confess now wasn't one of them with recent events. But today, they decided was going to be exciting, it deserved to start with a bang, in the nicest sense of the word.

Jamie announced they needed to hurry up if they were to be on time. They were supposed to be meeting Bonnie in Exeter midmorning, and Claire wanted to do some last-minute Christmas shopping in the big city. Jamie shouldn't have tempted her to stay in bed. Now they would be late, and that wasn't a good start.

Today was a momentous day for all three of them and much anticipated. Still savouring the warmth of the bed, Claire and Jamie scrambled to get dressed and disappeared with a slam of the front door. Englebert was home for the day. At the cold blast of air which followed their departure, he promptly took himself back to bed hunkering deep under the duvet.

Claire and Jamie had spoken to Bonnie a lot since reconnecting and this was the next step. Claire was trying to remain calm as best she could, but this was a big deal. When Bonnie had suggested the get-together half-way between Bristol and Cornwall, they jumped at the idea. Now, none of them could believe it was happening. Claire knew it would take time to adjust to reality, and there was no pressure on any of them. They would take each step one day at a time. They had the rest of their lives ahead of them.

Bonnie had never expected to get back in touch with her parents. She thought it would be a dream come true if it happened, and now it was. Bonnie wasn't naïve in expecting everything to be perfect. She knew the perfect family didn't exist, especially in her profession as a lawyer. But this was the opportunity she had been waiting for. She left Bristol early, wanting to beat the Saturday traffic. She had been too excited to sleep and had woken up in the early hours and watched a film instead. Now as Bonnie waited in front of Exeter Cathedral, she looked worried, mixed with other emotions. She had waited a long time for this day, and now it was finally happening.

Claire spotted their daughter first. She looked just like Claire in her younger days. Giddy with excitement, they hugged and kissed and held each other. Jamie suggested that Claire and Bonnie spend some quality time together shopping. Jamie had a couple of errands he wanted to do alone, and they agreed to meet at the bistro on the square. Arm in arm, the two women wandered off chatting.

Jamie couldn't be happier; the two women he loved most in the world together. Life was turning out just fine. He loved the outdoors and was looking forward to moving to the beach and most of all, living with Claire. This was the icing on the cake.

Lunch turned out to be a raving success. Claire and Jamie questioned Bonnie about her love life, which she claimed was non-existent. Jamie couldn't understand why she hadn't been snatched up. She was a beautiful, normal, happy woman except when she talked about the law. Then she was totally serious.

Bonnie told them about her little house. It wasn't much, but it was her home, and she loved her own space. Especially after her working week. It was nice to wound down. She enjoyed painting when she could with watercolours and reading. 'I'm not much of a cook,' she confessed. Jamie laughed as Bonnie mentioned it. Like mother, like daughter.

Claire and Jamie listened and heard the pain beneath Bonnie's words. Nobody was better placed to understand the pain of loss, they had all suffered when they had been separated from each other. They cried, and they laughed, and they cried some more. There was just so much to say in such a short time.

Claire thought it was remarkable how one individual action could trigger a sequence of events. With such far-reaching consequences, some of which wouldn't become obvious until much later in all their lives.

Jamie remembered when he first met Claire. He thought she was the most beautiful girl he had ever seen, a knockout. She still was as Jamie looked at both women. Bonnie and Claire were so alike.

Claire and Jamie were full of admiration for Bonnie. She deeply appreciated what they said, validating the decisions she had made and the life she had chosen. Bonnie smiled warmly at her parent's kind words. They were so proud of what she had accomplished and the world she lived in. She had managed to stay real despite it all.

'My adopted family would disown me if I didn't, she said honestly. Maybe that's what keeps me true to myself. I have to face them, and myself at some point. And now you. They both laughed at what Bonnie said.

Bonnie promised she would come down for Christmas. She wanted to see the funny little beach town where they lived. There was something so restorative about the ocean. They talked about it over lunch, and Jamie and Claire were thrilled Bonnie was coming. They really liked each other and anybody watching them would have thought they had known each forever. Bonnie felt surprisingly comfortable with her parents, considering they had only met that morning. She sensed quickly that they were to be trusted, and they felt the same way about her.

They all appreciated the openness and honesty between them as they laid some of the past to rest. It had been a long time coming.

They didn't want the day to end. As they went in opposite directions, they all knew it would only be for a short time. Sometimes you just knew when it was right, and when it was for real. They had never felt this way before or been this sure that they would spend the rest of their lives together as a family.

This was the daughter Claire and Jamie had been waiting for, the family chink they had been missing. They needed each other in their lives. And for all three of them, this was the magic they had dreamed of and thought they wouldn't find. Everything was going to be alright.

For the first time, they were a complete family.

Chapter Fifty-Nine

While Claire Cornish was playing happy families with her fiancé and their daughter at Christmas, Danielle Butler was in Paris savouring the City of Light alone. She watched couples laughing and eating in the cafes and walking along the illuminated boulevards. The capital invited you to fall in love and the promise of an unforgettable Christmas. For Danielle Butler, the timeless, romantic city reminded her of what she could have back in Cornwall. This Christmas would be remembered for all the right reasons. It would be her last Christmas on her own.

Danielle Butler flipped through her tablet, reading the online version of the Cornish Guardian, flipping through the contents until she found what she was looking for. She knew the words off by heart. The story was the main feature covering the Devon and Cornwall Police cases throughout that year and highlighting one person, in particular, DCI Claire Cornish. Spectacular results had been achieved, and Chief Constable Jane Falconbridge extolled the virtues of her staff and especially DCI Cornish. DCS Butler was briefly mentioned, but the main photograph was of her nemesis, Claire Cornish.

By the new year, the story would have disappeared and be forgotten. But for Danielle Butler, it wasn't. She relaxed and thought back over the years. She might have foolishly misjudged Cornish and been outsmarted by her.

Danielle Butler smiled. That wouldn't happen again, Jamie Nance belonged to her.

Chapter Sixty

Claire took out her car keys. The call of the crime scene had dragged her from her bed. By some miracle, she had managed to spend Christmas with Jamie and Bonnie but with it was too much to hope for a quiet New Year.

Seagulls screeched noisily overhead, breaking her train of thought. It was dark out, the inky night sky looking like a sombre canopy. Low cloud cover was a deep-blue-grey that matched the hues of the tarmac road. She hoped it wasn't an omen for what was to come. Just what she needed tonight. A double murder on New Year's Eve.

Claire would be relieved to see the back of this year although there had been some high points, namely the reconnection with their daughter, Bonnie. Claire had been pleased to hear that Bonnie's childhood had been a happy one. All too often adopted children ended up living in disjointed families which would have further compounded Claire's guilt. She was grateful her daughter had emerged an unscathed adult. The very thought of Bonnie made Claire smile as she drove along the country lanes. That was what unconditional love felt like; overwhelming.

Christmas had been a blessing for all of them, and Claire was looking forward to all the Easters, birthdays, summer holidays and the general get-togethers in the future. They had even talked of Bonnie working with her father in the future. But for now, they were happy to let life progress at its natural pace.

Claire hadn't planned on being launched straight into another murder enquiry quite so soon. She had hoped for a tractor or car theft or even a simple burglary.

As she approached the blue and white police cordon tape, Claire looked at the mish-mash of buildings in various stages of decay. The business and buildings were on a prime spot of land ripe for redevelopment in the right hands. Claire was thinking about what kind of human being attacked and killed two elderly people? Some people were right bastards.

Cornish parked up and reached DC Mac, who was already manning the police cordon and crime scene.

'Evening ma'am, I was first on the scene,' Mac said, looking pale and shocked at having discovered the murder victims.

'Are you okay?' Cornish asked.

'It's not a pretty sight. Oh, and Happy New Year ma'am,' replied Mac as an afterthought.

'I'm sure,' replied Cornish as she stepped into the arena once more to thwart a killer.

The End

Cover design copyright © FG Laycy

ISBN: 9798646799457

Imprint: Independently published

Author's Note

I wrote this novel during a time none of us will ever forget. That of the lockdown and COVID-19, coronavirus in 2020. I happened to be in lockdown in a chalet named Skylark in Gwithian Sands, having just sold my house. Which is why I decided to include the chalet and Gwithian Sands in my book.

This period in all of our lives has proved not only challenging but inspirational. People have shown their real strengths in their behaviour and outlook. Ordinary people have raised millions for the NHS and other charities, and one man deserves a special mention, Captain Sir Thomas Moore. And there are plenty of others. Too many to name, and the clapping for carers has helped the NHS staff feel loved and appreciated as the British public show their support for the NHS workers on the front line of the coronavirus pandemic.

Our lives have changed for now and possibly forever. The future will be different, with hopefully less air travel and freedom of movement around the world. This may, in turn, restore the balance with nature and bring people back to a simpler life, including simple pleasures such as reading more and appreciating what we have.

This book is very much a work of fiction and is set in spectacular Cornwall. The county has provided inspiration for me and my writing. Once we are out of this pandemic safely, it is hoped that people will enjoy the wonders of Cornwall once more. There is something magical about this beautiful place, and I never tire of watching the sea.

The names of places have been preserved to bring a realistic licence to my stories and to honestly describe the wonderful and really beautiful qualities that Cornwall has to offer. However, my characters are fictitious and any resemblance to real persons, living or dead, is purely coincidental.

Fiona

Bio

F G Laycy is the author behind the DCI Claire Cornish Mystery Novels, the Hunter Mackenzie series and standalone romance novels.

Born in Kenilworth, Warwickshire, Fiona moved to Worcester and Coventry to train and become a State Registered Nurse. After working in nursing for many years, she moved to Russia with her family. She remained there for eleven years before relocating to Cornwall.

She now divides her time between Cornwall and France.

Books by Fiona

F G Laycy

Hunter Mackenzie series:

The Tenth Congress

The Day of Reckoning

F G Laycy

DCI Claire Cornish Mystery Novels:

Carrick Roads

Highcliff

13 Falmouth Road

Fiona Laycy

Romance Novels:

Maybe, One Day

The full-length novels are all available to purchase in e-book and paperback on the Amazon store.

Please leave a review

I do hope anyone who takes the time to read my books will leave a review. It will be very much appreciated.

Writing is my passion, and I would like to think that each book is an enjoyable read. It's a process that every writer wants to improve, but we don't always get it right. And we can't please every reader.

Kind words can transform the lives of those that give and those that receive.

Thanks

Fiona

Printed by Amazon Italia Logistica S.r.l.
Torrazza Piemonte (TO), Italy

16370924R00169